Blood Rite

Also by E.J. Stevens

Ivy Granger World

Ivy Granger
Urban Fantasy Series

Frostbite
Shadow Sight
Blood and Mistletoe
Ghost Light
Club Nexus
Burning Bright
Devil in the Details
Birthright
Hound's Bite
Thrill on Joysen Hill
Blood Rite
Tales from Harborsmouth

Hunters' Guild
Urban Fantasy Series

Hunting in Bruges

Spirit Guide
Young Adult Series

She Smells the Dead
Spirit Storm
Legend of Witchtrot Road
Brush with Death
The Pirate Curse

Whitechapel Paranormal Society
Victorian Horror, Gaslamp Fantasy

Craven Street

IVY GRANGER PSYCHIC DETECTIVE

Blood Rite

E.J. STEVENS

Published by Sacred Oaks Press
Sacred Oaks, 221 Sacred Oaks Lane, Wells, Maine 04090

First Printing (trade paperback edition), July 2016

Stevens, E.J.
Hound's Bite/ E.J. Stevens

ISBN 978-0-9894887-9-2 (trade pbk.)

Printed in the United States of America

PUBLISHER'S NOTE
This is a work of fiction. Names, characters, places, and
incidents either are the product of the author's imagination or
are used fictitiously, and any resemblance to actual persons,
living or dead, business establishments, events, or locales is
entirely coincidental.

PRONUNCIATION GUIDE

Pronunciations are given phonetically for names and races found in the Ivy Granger series. Alternate names and nicknames have been provided in parentheses. In some cases, the original folklore has been changed to suit the city of Harborsmouth and its environs.

Ailinn: ah-lynn
Aleya: uh-LEE-yuh
Arachne: uh-RAK-nee
Athame: ah-thaw-may
Banshee: ban-shee (Bean Sidhe, Bean Sìth)
Barguest: BAR-guyst (Bargheist, Black Dog)
Bean Tighe: ban tig
Béchuille: beh-huh-IL (Bé Chuille)
Bema: BEE-muh
Bheur: ver (like air)
Blaosc: BLEE-usk
Bogey: BOH-gee
Boggart: BOG-ert
Boitata: boy-TAH-ta
Brollachan: broll-ach-HAWN
Brownie: BROW-nee (Bwca, Urisk, Hearth Faerie, Domestic Hobgoblin)
Bugbear: BUG-bayr (Bug-a-boo, Boggle-bo)
Bwca: BOO-kuh (see Brownie)
The Cailleach: kall-ahk (The Blue Hag, Cailleach Bheur, Queen of Winter, Crone, Veiled One, Winter Hag)
Cat Sidhe: KAT shee or kayth shee (Faerie Cat, Cait Shith, Cait Sith)
Ceffyl Dŵr: keff-EEL dore (Kelpie King, Ceff)
Chir batti: CHEER bhut-TEA
Clurichaun: kloor-ih-kon (clobhair)
Cu Sith: KOO shee
Daeva: DAY-va
Demon: DEE-mun

Djinn: JIN
Draugr: DROW-ger
Duergar: doER-gar
Each Uisge: erk OOSH-kuh (Water Horse)
Elphame: EL-faym
Emain Ablach: EH-van ah-BLAH
Faerie: FAIR-ee (Fairy, Sidhe, Fane, Wee Folk, The Gentry,
People of Peace, Themselves, Sidhe, Fae, Fay, Good Folk)
Fear Dearg: far DAR-rig (The Red Man)
Fionn mac Cumhaill: FIN mac COO-will
Forneus: FOR-nee-us (Demon, Great Marquis of Hell)
Fragarach: FRAG ah roch
Fuath: FOO-ah
Gaius Aurelius: GUY-us aw-REE-lee-us
Galliel: GAL-ee-el (Unicorn)
Ghoul: GOOL (Revenant)
Glaistig: GLASS-tig (The Green Lady)
Gnome: NOHM
Goblin: GOB-lin
Griffin: GRIF-fin (Gryphon, Griffon)
Grindylow: GRIN-dee-loh
Gwarwyn-a-throt: GWAR-win-uh-THROT
Gwynn ap Nudd: gwin-AP-need
Hamadryad: ha-ma-DRY-ad (Tree Nymph)
Harborsmouth: HAR-bers-MOUTH
Henkie: HEN-kee
Hippocampus: hip-po-CAM-pus
Hob-o-Waggle HOB-oh-WAG-gul (Brownie, son of Wag-at-the-
Wa)
Hy Brasil: HY bra-ZIL
Ignus fatuus: IG-nus FATCH-you-us
Inari: i-NAH-ree
Jenny Greenteeth: JEN-nee GREEN-teeth (Water Hag)
Kelpie: KEL-pee (Water Horse, Nyaggle)
Lamia: LAY-me-uh
Leanansídhe: lan-awn-shee (Lhiannan Sidhe, Leanhaun Shee,
Leannan Sìth, Fairy Mistress)
Leprechaun: le-pre-khan (leipreachán)
Loup garou: LOOP guh-ROO
Mab: MAB (Unseelie Queen)

Manannán mac Lir: MAH-nah-nahn mac leer
Mauthe doog: MOW-thee DOO
Melusine: MEL-oo-seen
Mermaid: MER-mayd (male Merman)
Merry Dancer: MER-ree DAN-ser (Fir Chlis)
Murúch: mer-ook (Merrow, Moruadh, Murúghach)
Nixie: NIX-ee
Nuckelavees: NOOK-uh-LAY-veez
Oberon: OH-ber-on (Seelie King)
Peg Powler: PEG POW-ler (Peg Powler of the Trees, Water Hag)
Peri: PER-ee
Pixie: PIK-see (Pisgie)
Pooka: POO-kuh (Phooka, Pouka, Púca, Pwca)
Redcap: RED-kap (red cap)
Roca Barraidh: ROH-ka BAR-rah
Saytr: SAY-ter
Selkie: SEL-kee
Shellycoat: SHEL-lee-cote
Sidhe: SHEE (see Faerie)
Succubus: SUK-you-bus (male Incubus)
Tech Duinn: tek DOON
Tezcatlipocan: tehs-cah-tlee-poh-cahn
Tir na nOg: TEER na NOHG
Tir Tairngire: TEER TEARN-geer
Titania: ti-TAY-nee-uh (Seelie Queen)
Troll: TROHL
Tuatha Dé Danann: tootha DAY da-NAN
Tylwyth Teg: TILL-with TEEG (Seelie Court)
Unicorn: YOU-ni-korn
Unseelie: un-SEE-lee
Vampire: VAM-pyr (Undead)
Will-o'-the-Wisp: WIL-oh-tha-wisp (Gyl Burnt Tayle, Jack o' Lantern, Wisp, Ghost Light, Friar's Lantern, Corpse Candle, Hobbledy, Aleya, Hobby Lantern, Chir Batti, Faerie Fire, Spunkies, Min Min Light, Luz Mala, Pinket, Ellylldan, Spook Light, Ignus Gatuus, Orbs, Boitatá, and Hinkypunk)
Ynis Afallon: un-NIS AH-fuhl-on
Yue Fei: yweh-fay

And, on thy blade and dudgeon, gouts of blood,
Which was not so before. There's no such thing:
It is the bloody business which informs,
Thus to mine eyes. Now o'er the one half-world
Nature seems dead, and wicked dreams abuse...
—Shakespeare, MacBeth

INTRODUCTION

Welcome to Harborsmouth, where monsters walk the streets unseen by humans...except those with second sight.

Whether visiting our modern business district or exploring the cobblestone lanes of the Old Port quarter, please enjoy your stay. When you return home, do tell your friends about our wonderful city—just leave out any supernatural details.

Don't worry—most of our guests never experience anything unusual. Otherworlders, such as faeries, vampires, and ghouls, are quite adept at hiding within the shadows. Many are also skilled at erasing memories. You may wake in the night screaming, but you won't recall why. Be glad that you don't remember—you are one of the fortunate ones.

If you do encounter something unnatural, we recommend the services of Ivy Granger, Psychic Detective. Co-founder of Private Eye detective agency, Ivy Granger is a relatively new member of our small business community. Her offices can be found on Water Street, in the heart of the Old Port.

Miss Granger has a remarkable ability to receive visions by the act of touching an object. This skill is useful in her detective work, especially when locating lost items. Whether you are looking for a lost brooch or missing persons, no job is too small for Ivy Granger—and she could certainly use the business.

We can also provide, upon request, a list of highly skilled undertakers. If you are in need of their services, then we also kindly direct you to Harborsmouth Cemetery Realty. It's never too early to contact them, since we have a booming "housing" market. Demand is quite high for a local plot—there are always people *dying* for a place to stay.

CHAPTER 1

I smiled, looking out our loft window at the sun peeking from between the clouds. After days of rainy weather, Harborsmouth glittered as sunbeams hit the glistening buildings. Sparky would be able to go play in the park that had sprung up from our battle with the Wild Hunt. It had been days since he rode on Marvin's shoulders or learned new pixing tricks from Hob.

I scooped up the bowl of soggy cereal from the windowsill and walked it to our kitchen sink, one gloved hand absently reaching up to tug at the huge snarl of pixie locks I'd woken up with. I should be mad at Hob for teaching my kid to be a total rascal, but I was too damn happy. If you'd told me a year ago that the worst my nights would throw at me were hobgoblin pranks and dirty dishes, I'd have stabbed you.

Glancing out the window at the glittering rooftops, my smile widened. It's funny how things change.

The city had settled into a new rhythm. Instead of being hunted by hellhounds, eaten by slavering water fae, or battling pyromaniacal imps, I was working simple, straightforward cases and coming home to my family. The fact that my new family included a gorgeous kelpie king and an adorable demon child made my breath hitch.

How could I, Ivy Granger, daughter of the Queen of Air and Darkness, be allowed such happiness? How, after all that I'd learned and all that our city had been through, could I think that we'd ever be safe?

The truth was, I didn't believe it, not at first. I saw threats everywhere. But it's not paranoia if they're really out to get you, right? At least, that's what I quipped to Jinx so often, she threatened to have it stitched onto our wedding invitations.

Yes, stitched. Jinx's current obsession, beyond increasing our office's efficiency and reminding me to eat, was embroidered linen invitations. I shook my head with a snort. My best friend was going overboard with wedding planning.

Our weddings, plural.

That brought a brief frown to my face followed by the inevitable goofy grin. The idea of marriage still made my skin itch, but it also made me ridiculously happy. I suppose that was the point, at least for what I still thought of as my human side. For the fae, such a union meant much more. In addition to happiness, a marriage oath was a bond that solidified alliances and guaranteed protection for my loved ones.

It also would make my demon child—no, really, he had come from Hell and been trapped in a witch vessel that held a horde of fire imps, until Arachne had dropped the vessel and set them all free—a prince. Sparky, my adorable, floppy-eared, little guy, would become second in line to the kelpie throne, right behind his adoptive daddy, Ceffyl Dwr. I really hoped that Ceff knew what he was doing.

Not that logic and faerie bargains were all that mattered. It did feel right to make Sparky officially family.

Even Jinx bringing Forneus into our found family was beginning to feel like pairing peppermint with our chocolate, although I'd never tell him that. Our adversarial barbs had turned to a playful sniping that I'd miss if we got all mushy. Forneus had gone from enemy to really ancient older brother, the kind who puts spiders in your bed. Actually, it was the other way around. Maybe, Hob isn't the only one teaching my kid to be a little trickster.

I glanced over to where Sparky snored, curled up in the dog bed beside our tattered sofa. It was hard to believe he'd only come into my life mere months ago.

Our family had grown. That scared me. Having so much to live for also meant that I had more to lose. The possibility of threats to Jinx, Ceff, Sparky, Hob, Marvin, Forneus, Galliel, Father Michael, Humphrey, Torn, Midnight, and especially Kaye now that my witch friend was vulnerable, kept me on high alert. I couldn't let them get hurt again. And I sure as hell couldn't lose them, any of them, ever.

But after weeks of jumping at shadows, and months of running emergency drills and implementing new security plans, I'd relaxed my guard. I'd let myself be lulled by the new peaceful state of my city and the growing sense of contentment that came with the bonds of friendship, the bloodshed of allies, and the blossoming of a love so true it made my head spin and lips tingle.

I'd started to focus on existing problems—solving cases, rebuilding The Emporium, fixing the hole Humphrey had put in our roof, and, Oberon help me, wedding planning—rather than worrying about the unknown. I'd stopped expecting new monsters to threaten our city and chewed on strategies to negotiate with the devils I knew. Heck, I even started thinking of some of my old enemies as, well, maybe not friends but potential allies.

In other words, I was a fool.

CHAPTER 2

I left the loft, escaping the heap of wedding invitation samples for the familiar chaos of our detective agency. Private Eye's offices were located beneath the loft apartment I still shared with Jinx, a situation that was becoming more and more crowded. The wedding planning samplers didn't help, not that I'd decided on what to do about it. Ceff wanted to get our own place, but I loathed anything new, or worse anything old, so I remained at the loft with Jinx, Ceff, Forneus, and Sparky, and Humphrey on his perch on our roof.

I waved to the gargoyle, who appeared to be a stone ornament to normal humans, and shouted, "how's it hangin'?" before reaching for our office door. That raised a few eyebrows, but the low rumble of Humphrey's laughter was worth it. I liked the kid and he provided an added layer of security that I appreciated. But I was also responsible for the gargoyle losing his home. The least I could do was let him roof surf until his home was repaired.

I had inadvertently given Kaye her full powers back, corruptible power that twisted my friend into someone I hardly recognized. Magic is funny that way. It requires balance, and a price. I'd screwed up that balance and my friend had betrayed us, and together we blew up her spell kitchen, along with her entire occult shop. Humphrey, Hob, and Midnight had lost their homes, and Kaye was lost inside her mind.

Losing oneself, becoming trapped inside your own head, was one of my greatest fears, right after losing any more of my loved ones. For me, it was a daily threat. The gift of psychometry is great for solving cases, but it has a steep downside. It's what faerie magic and witch magic have in common—it's all about the balance.

My psychic gift was one of the reasons I was bothered by the heap of wedding samples that cluttered our apartment. How many people had touched those things, and under what circumstances? The threat of touching those invitations and being pulled down into a terrible vision kept me from going near that corner of the loft. At least, that's what I told myself. There was also a tiny part of me that felt guilty for planning a happy future when so many still suffered.

I would fix things. I would rebuild The Emporium, help Kaye recover, and find a way to bring my father home, for good this time, but first I needed to make enough money to cover contractors, my friend's care, and deep research on breaking curses. For that, I took on the cases that nobody else would. To my surprise, I was damn good at it.

Humming a tune from one of Sparky's favorite cartoons, I opened the office door and entered Private Eye psychic detective agency. It was the smell that stopped me dead in my tracks, not that the skeletal face of the vampire sitting in our waiting room was much better. I nearly ran.

"Corpse candle," Sir Gaius said.

CHAPTER 3

I should have run. Listening to a dusty old vampire rattle on was torture. Not that bored was the prevailing mood. I don't think it's possible to be bored while gripping your blades so tight your knuckles audibly pop, even through thick leather gloves.

Jinx flashed me a worried frown, but I shook my head. I was fine. Everything was fine. We just had to survive the mood swings of a master vampire who was massively pissed off, but who was also easily ensnared by the minutia of his so-called harvesting rights.

Every time Gaius said the word harvesting, I puked a little in my mouth. He wasn't talking about crops or hay. What good would those things be to an ancient vampire? He was a slumlord with bony fingers in a multitude of properties around the city, including most of Joysen Hill, making him ridiculously wealthy and scarily powerful. But it was his treaties regarding blood and corpses that really got his dusty panties in a bunch.

Gaius was working himself up again, pounding his fist hard enough to crack the cheap waiting room chair that sat to his right. I was keeping a mental tally of everything he touched, and damaged, so that Jinx could bill him later. No way was I touching anything Gaius came into contact with, but breaking our furniture was just plain rude. Old vampires, the truly ancient ones like Sir Gaius, usually kept a stronger leash on their emotions and honored the long-standing traditions of hospitality.

Not today.

The fact that Gaius was coming unglued over such a small matter either meant I was missing something here or he was beginning the final deterioration that took the extremely undead. Neither option was comforting.

"...blah, blah, blah, legal MUMBO JUMBO!" he hissed.

Okay, that's not really what he said, but my brain was starting to shift into survival mode, focusing on the vampire's tone and body language rather than his words.

Gaius' voice was beginning to rise again, gaining a sibilant shriek as his fangs elongated and he started to lose control of his anger. That was my cue. Jinx had been trying to diffuse the situation with lots of questions about the aforesaid treaties, a tactic that proved she was the brains of our little business, but that could only stall the vampire for so long. He was starting to froth at the mouth, a stomach-churning pink-tinged dust forming at the corners of his lips, a sure sign that we needed to end this, now, or at least get his attention off my tasty human business partner.

"What do you want me to do about it?" I asked.

"How dare you interrupt..." he sputtered.

His eye sockets flashed, but I held my ground. Yeah, I don't know how he does it either. Apparently, it's a vampire thing. What I did know was that Gaius was extremely, massively, seriously pissed off. I wanted him out of my office and away from Jinx, like, yesterday.

"You came into my territory, threatened my vassal, and vandalized my property," I said, forcing more confidence and conviction into the words than I felt. My voice didn't shake once. Go, me. "It's high time you got to the point of your visit, Gaius. What. Do. You. Want?"

I bit off the words then held my breath. That middle bit was a stretch. Jinx was my human vassal, a title I hated but that gave her access to places humans weren't normally allowed to enter and kept most fae from messing with her, but claiming that Gaius had threatened her was splitting hairs. But I'd spent a lot of time amongst predators and one thing they had in common was body language.

Gaius flashing his fangs, swiftly growing fangs, didn't just telegraph his emotional state. In the supernatural world, that could be perceived as a threat. It was a dubious claim, but a claim nonetheless. In addition to your garden variety predators, I'd been sharing my apartment with a demon attorney. Apparently, I'd picked up a thing or two from Forneus' legal rants.

Gaius went unnaturally still. My lungs hurt from holding my breath, and I wished that the master vampire would go back to breaking my furniture.

Jinx reached for her crossbow, and my hand slid to the wooden stakes at the small of my back, but we were too late. Gaius lunged, fangs erupting from froth-covered lips.

My utility belt and Jinx's desk had never seemed so far away. Even with my faerie-enhanced reflexes, the vampire was faster. It was like moving through molasses, or congealed blood. I pulled energy from the city's ley lines, the magic making my teeth hum painfully as if I was biting on a power line, and something tore inside of me.

Whatever it was, I'd worry about it later. If there was a later. Gaius was fast, damn fast, and he was pissed.

Most of the skills I'd learned in Faerie applied here in the human world, but they were much harder to manifest. According to Ceff, that was because in Faerie magic was everywhere. Here in the mortal world, I had to make do with the weaker magic that flowed naturally or steal it from a source, in this case the ley lines, that I shouldn't have direct access to. Nobody, not even Ceff, really understood how I did that. But we all agreed it should be reserved as a last resort.

That logic went out the window went a master vampire lunged toward my best friend. Gritted teeth vibrating and bones aching, I thrust my hand out, fingers twisting in an arcane gesture. Gaius stopped, eye sockets widening in what might have been fear. Whatever the emotion, he took a step back, hands out to his sides.

Vampires, at least the ones with any survival instinct, are terrified of fire. For good reason. As vampires age, they shrivel up, like a dry, mummified, prune-like husk. It's why older vamps lack the softer bits, losing ears, eyes, and nose. Those are always the first to go. It's also why they light up like a torch.

Good thing I was a wisp princess with the ability to create the occasional fireball and, with the help of a ley line or two, a controlled wall of flame. Control of course was key. The last thing I needed was to save Jinx only to burn down our home and business. Was Sparky awake yet? Would fire harm a baby demon?

My stomach clenched and I let go of the ley lines and sent the wall of flame back where it came from. Sweat beaded on my upper lip, but since Gaius' shriveled lips were still covered in pink-tinged froth, I didn't worry too much about it.

I also forced my hands away from my ribs where I was pretty sure I'd torn open an old injury. A lamia, Ceff ex-wife, had left a mass of scar tissue there when she'd sunk her venomous fangs into my flank and tried to kill me. The wound had healed but left a weak spot. Not that I had time for physical weak spots at the moment. Gaius was starting to twitch and his head snapped over to growl at Jinx who was still reaching for her crossbow.

"Touch her and I will burn you to ash, hoover you, leave you in a vacuum bag for all eternity, and you will never find out who's stealing your bloody corpses," I said.

"Who said they were bloody?" he asked.

Good, his attention was on me. I gave Jinx the slightest wave of my hand, hoping she'd put her desk, and her crossbow, between her and Gaius.

"It was a turn of phrase," I said.

"So, you will take the case, little corpse candle?" he asked. "You will discover who is using necromancy to raise sesquithialchthiliadians from the pet cemetery and encroaching on my harvesting rights..."

He was getting agitated again, and I did not want a repeat of our showdown. I didn't think I could pull from a ley line again today, not yet anyway, and I didn't think I could stake Gaius before he tore off my head. That would leave Jinx on her own. So, I did the only thing that I could.

"I'll take the case," I said.

"Swear it," he said.

Gaius was a smart bastard. Damn him to hell.

"I swear it," I said.

I gasped, the faerie bargain settling like a lead weight on my shoulders. I blinked rapidly, but with a flash of fang and a final muttering about harvesting rights, Gaius was gone.

A papyrus scroll dropped to the floor and pink dust hung in the air. The bloody dust motes were a disgusting reminder of the vampire's anger.

I shoved two earplugs up my nose faster than you can say, vision from hell. At least faerie-fast reflexes were good for something. Jinx was slower, but her solution was even better. She tossed me a dust mask, the disposable kind, and ran for the vacuum.

CHAPTER 4

Grave robbing is Harborsmouth's second best-kept secret. The first is the existence of supernatural creatures that live alongside the city's humans. In fact, the dirtiest little secret of all might be the truth behind most of those empty graves.

Most supernaturals eke out a pretty mundane existence. We go to work and, on a good week, we pay the bills that keep the lights on and a roof over our heads. Nobody wants a return to the Burning Times.

Well, nobody sane.

The creature that was stealing the more odiferous of Harborsmouth's citizens from their graves had to be crazy.

Sir Gaius, ruler of the local vamps, owned the harvesting rights to every corpse buried within the city limits. No one touched the vampire master of the city's property without permission and lived to scream about it—until now.

But some supernaturals, especially the older more feral vampires and malicious, carnivorous faeries, don't stick to the rules that keep us one step ahead of a potential war.

I shivered. War. That one word thrust images unbidden into my mind, nightmarish landscapes filled with the fallen, the doomed, the damned. If war broke out between the supernaturals and humans, the streets of Harborsmouth would run red—and blue, black, purple, and green—with the blood of innocents.

Worse, I knew that war was on the horizon.

Our friend Jenna Lehane and our new ally Master Janus of the Hunters' Guild had both warned of an inevitable war brewing between those extremist supernaturals and the humans they viewed as food. According to Jenna, the anarchist vampires and faeries were amassing power by stealing arcane artifacts and religious relics from around the globe. Jenna and her team were tasked with thwarting those thefts, at times even performing thrilling heists to take possession of the power items before our enemies, but it would take more than the Hunters' Guild to stop this war.

And over all my nightmarish imaginings of what that war would bring, stood the figure of a goddess of old. For no matter who won the battle, The Morrigan is always the victor in war. Like the raptors and the carrion birds of which she could take the form of, The Morrigan thrived on death and the corpses of the fallen.

"Zombie gerbils," Jinx said, dispelling all thoughts of The Morrigan.

"Um, what?" I asked.

Oh, right. The inciting incident that might bring about our doom. Someone, or something, had used a form of sorcery to raise a bunch of gerbil-like fae from a local pet cemetery. When I pictured the end of the world, that was one scenario I never even considered.

"Zombie gerbils," Jinx said, shaking her head.

She wasn't the only one. Now that Gaius was gone and the worst of his stink removed from our office, his words were starting to sink in.

"I guess we could call them zombie faeries that look like gerbils, but, yeah, zombie gerbils," I said. "It's a hell of a lot easier to say, and explain, than reanimated sesquithialchthiliadians."

"We almost died because of zombie gerbils," she said.

"Well, to be fair, Gaius was pissed about someone stealing the corpses," I said. "I'm not so sure he even cares that there are zombie gerbils running around the city."

"HARVESTING RIGHTS," Jinx intoned with her nose in the air, holding the pose until she dissolved into a fit of giggles.

"Gross," I said, struggling to keep a straight face.

"Mega gag," she said, wiping her eyes between giggles. "We almost died."

"Over an Oberon-be-damned pet cemetery," I said, biting my lip.

I tried not to laugh, but Jinx's giggling was contagious. It took me a few minutes to get my breathing under control.

"How did faeries end up in a pet cemetery?" Jinx asked.

Now that was a sobering thought.

"That's a good question," I said. "I'll find out. If someone is enslaving fae as exotic pets, we need to stop them."

"After we catch the zombie gerbils and find whoever dug them up, stealing them from Gaius," she said.

"After catching zombie gerbils," I muttered, rubbing a gloved hand over my face. "How is this my life?"

"You love it and you know it," she said.

"True that," I said.

"Weirdo," she said.

"Also true," I said with a shrug.

"Want some coffee before your great gerbil hunt?" she asked.

I grinned from ear to ear. After a week of rain, the sun was shining. I had a case that paid well and probably wouldn't kill me, and my best friend was offering me coffee. Maybe, this was a good day after all.

"Hell, yes," I said.

"Good," she said with a wink. "Before you leave, I need you go over Gaius' contract. We might even want to consult a professional before you sign."

Jinx blushed, eyes going dreamy, and I knew exactly who she thought we should consult. So much for my good day.

CHAPTER 5

I'd come around to the idea of my best friend dating a demon attorney, but that didn't mean I enjoyed listening to Forneus drone on about legal terminology and contract loopholes as if they were the most fascinating thing ever.

Forneus was insisting we make changes, in blood, before signing Gaius' contract. I'd already agreed to take the case, to find out who was encroaching on the master vampires harvesting rights. That bargain sat heavy on me, giving me a headache. I needed to get moving.

But Forneus was right. I had agreed to take the case, and of course I needed to find out who was stealing corpses in my city, but blindly signing a contract with the undead was foolish at best.

It didn't help that Benmore showed up in the middle of our discussion, impatiently asking for the signed contract. Benmore might be mayor of the city, but we all knew who ruled Harborsmouth's supernatural underbelly. The dwarf was little more than Gaius' errand boy, something I continued to tell myself as I tried repeatedly not to shoot, or stab, the messenger.

"You'll the get the contract when we're good and ready," I grumbled.

"But, m'lady," Benmore said.

"Not one second sooner," I said, narrowing my eyes.

It was all I could do not to bare my teeth, but, just as I could claim a flash of fang was a threat to my vassal, Gaius could take the gesture as a direct threat. That was a complication we didn't need.

Benmore's beard twitched in frustration, and I turned back to Forneus with a growl. To say I was grouchy was an understatement. The morning sunbeams promising fair weather had been a lie. The renewed rainstorm was a bad omen that set my teeth on edge. The incessant drip-drip-plop of water into the bucket behind my desk was also a constant reminder of our current financial crisis.

We were running Private Eye on a flea market shoestring that had seen more secondhand stores than a stack of TV Guides. We'd recently more than doubled the number of mouths we had to feed and now, after a week of nonstop rain, our roof was leaking.

And don't even get me started on the estimated cost of our upcoming double wedding. Oberon's eyes. How did I get talked into a big wedding? Ceff and I should have eloped.

Drip-drip-plop.

My shoulders hunched and I gripped the pen so tight I could feel the crack of plastic through my heavy leather gloves. We needed the money, but nothing good ever came of working for vampires, not when they insisted on Byzantine legal contracts.

I eyed the papyrus scroll as if it were about to turn into a spider, or a venomous snake like the vampire who penned it—with blood, of course, because vampires.

Vampires are devious, diabolical, and have a penchant for drama. Oh, yeah, they were also creepy as hell and ruined my office furniture. Too bad they owned most of the city's real estate and, apparently, its dead.

"How do these harvesting rights work exactly?" I asked, ignoring Benmore and his angrily twitching beard.

"My liege has clearly stated…," Benmore said.

I cut him off with a gesture so sharp it could cut through iron. Not that I'd be touching iron these days. Just one more thing I was grumpy about.

"I want to hear Forneus' take on this," I said. Forneus preened and Jinx smiled at me, and I sighed. "Don't let it go to your heads."

We'd called in an expert. He was a demon attorney with a knack for contracts, whether they involved souls or not. He was also my best friend's fiancé. My life had gone from weird to OH MY GOD FAIRY TALES ARE TRUE in the span of a year. And now here I was asking advice from the very demon who'd given us the Mab-be-damned case that had started it all.

I pinched the bridge of my nose, fending off a whopper of a headache.

"Forneus?" I asked, waving a hand. "Today would be nice. In case you haven't noticed, I've got a case to solve and a roof to fix."

"The short version, baby," Jinx said.

"Yes, my love," he said, kissing her hand. "As you wish."

"Today?" I asked.

Benmore fidgeted with his pocket watch and nodded anxiously.

"Fine, the short version is that Sir Gaius owns every corpse buried within the city limits," Forneus said. "While I could go on at length with theories as to why he might need such raw materials for constructing ghouls or creating new vampires, the fact remains that no matter his reasons, he owns the physical bodies of our dead."

"Not the souls," I said.

"No," Forneus said. "That is more my domain."

I frowned but I was determined not to get distracted. Forneus and I could have that conversation later. And make no mistake, there would be a discussion.

"And there's nothing in there about him raising zombies, or anyone raising zombies," I said.

I pinched the bridge of my nose. With the exception of the bodies raised when the Danse Macabre had been combined with a rare item from Hell, I wasn't aware that zombies even existed in real life. I'd always thought of them as a figment from my nightmares, the boogey man hiding the bed.

"No, as far as I'm aware, that type of necromancy is frowned upon," he said.

"And it's not really the issue here," I said, the pieces sliding into place. "Not for Gaius."

"If it was, I believe the vampire master would have participated more directly in taking down The Piper," he said, echoing my own thoughts. "I would wager that he did not care about the animation of those corpses because The Piper never removed them from their burial grounds."

"Only made them dance and tormented fae children in the process," I said, crushing another pen.

"Precisely," he said.

"Fine," I said, nodding to Forneus. "Make any necessary changes to cover my butt legally, and make sure my bargain is fulfilled once I find out who is encroaching on his harvesting rights."

"You'll need to inform Gaius personally," he said.

"Will a phone call count?" I asked.

"Yes," he said.

"Good," I said. "Just show me where to sign. This bargain is giving me a headache."

To his credit, Forneus had the final contract in front of me within the hour. I'm pretty sure that was a new record.

"You will need to sign in blood," Forneus said. "But I recommend you do not touch the parchment. I made addendums, but this page is the original."

And had been touched by an ancient vampire. Got it. I drew a dagger from my boot, pierced the pad of my thumb, and squeezed a few drops of blood onto document. I used a piece of a broken pen to sign my name, smearing my blood in a disgusting mockery of my signature. I swallowed hard and tossed the pen in the trash with a mental note to take the bin out in the alley and set it on fire.

"Are we done?" I asked.

"Yes," Forneus said, turning to Gaius' emissary. "Here you are, Benmore. Make haste."

"Aye, of course, haste indeed," the dwarf said, grabbing the contract.

Benmore backed out the door, bowing and thanking me as he went. If I heard someone call me "m'lady" one more time, I'd scream, or burn something, or stab someone.

But I'd kept my composure, as much as I'm able, remaining professional until the dwarf and Gaius' bloody contract was well out of my office. Then I turned to see my best friend and her betrothed making out against the file cabinets.

"Oberon's eyes, you two," I said. "Get a room."

Jinx pressed harder into Forneus and he deepened his kiss. I pretend gagged—it didn't take much acting skill since I was halfway to losing my breakfast—and rolled my eyes. After one more prolonged kiss, Jinx stepped away and Forneus pressed her hand to his lips.

"Later, my beloved," he said.

He bowed, much more elegantly than the dwarf had, and swept toward the door.

"Stay," I said. Forneus and Jinx both raised as eyebrow at me as if it was now a synchronized sport. I winced and forced a smile. "Please?"

"Since you asked so nicely, Miss Granger, I will delay my departure," Forneus said, a grin tugging at his lips.

Jinx nodded, biting her lower lip to keep from laughing.

"Har har har, keep that up and I'll stick spiders in your bed," I said.

"I knew that was you!" Jinx said with a snort.

I shrugged. I couldn't tell an outright lie. That didn't mean I had to answer the question. I was getting good at this faerie princess stuff.

Jinx was laughing, but Forneus looked less forgiving. I'd have to watch my back for the next few weeks. Hell, the long-lived had extensive memories and endless patience. I'd have to watch my back for eons.

I groaned at the realization that revenge could come at the demon's leisure, and Forneus winked. Great, just great.

"So, what's up?" Jinx asked.

"Besides zombie gerbils and Byzantine vampire blood contracts?" I asked.

"Yeah, yeah, besides that," she said, wiggling her fingers.

"As much as I want to go zombie hunting, heck, I need to go solve this case before my faerie blood starts to think I'm shirking the terms of my bargain, I think we need to talk this out," I said. "All of us."

"You believe more is going on than it appears," Forneus said.

"It's a possibility," I said. "We should be prepared. And I don't want to miss something because I was too stubborn to ask. I've learned a lot about faeries and the undead. I've even had a run-in with a necromancer, but there's still plenty I don't know."

"Team meeting?" Jinx asked.

"Family meeting," I said.

We may not be related by blood, but that didn't make it any less true. Sometimes you can pick your family and sometimes they pick you. Jinx had walked into my life and become my sister in every way that mattered. More recently, Ceff and Sparky had become a part of that family. Even Marvin, Hob, Kaye, Midnight, Humphrey, and Galliel had found a special place in my life and in my heart. I would do anything to keep them safe. Anything at all.

CHAPTER 6

For the sake of expediency, I did have a bargain hanging over my head after all, we decided to limit our family meeting to our housemates. I'd reach out to Marvin and Hob and the rest of our friends and allies soon enough, but, for now, our office held my best friend, a demon attorney, a gargoyle, a demon toddler, and an immortal kelpie king.

The fact that the kelpie king was bouncing the demon toddler on his knee and singing "Trot Trot to Boston" was an adorable bonus. Ceff's steady presence had a way of soothing my nerves no matter what he did, but his obvious love for Sparky was a reminder of what I had to live for and what I fought for. I'd become a hero, a role that caused a lot of crummy things to happen and a hell of a lot of loss, but seeing those two smiling, and being surrounded by my friends and housemates, made it all worthwhile.

I didn't want to shatter the moment of domestic bliss, but the clock was ticking.

"Jinx, did Gaius seem disproportionately angry to you?" I asked, mulling over the vampire's earlier visit.

Sir Gaius was never friendly, but he didn't usually commit vandalism. Ceff had already dragged the vampire-tainted furniture out behind the building where Humphrey broke it into kindling with one hand while Forneus and I had torched it, and my bloody trash bin, with magic flames while Sparky flicked his sparking fingers together. We were one big scary family.

Where the rest of us were scary powerful, Jinx was charming and clever. She was especially good when came to reading people. I sometimes wondered if that insight came from a subconscious awareness that most of the people in the room could crush her to a pulp or burn her to a crisp without even breaking a sweat.

Not that she was weak or defenseless. My friend was tough as nails and highly skilled with a crossbow, a weapon which she now absently touched from where it was slung over her shoulder. Jinx was a survivor.

"Oh, yeah," she said, nodding. "Gaius was definitely way more pissed off than he should have been. He usually walks around like he's got a stick up his butt, never showing any emotion at all. I kept thinking that he was taking this way too personal. I mean, come on, he was foaming at the mouth."

"Raaabies!" Sparky squealed, getting down on all fours and growling at Humphrey.

The gargoyle growled right back, the sound like a ton of bricks in a cement mixer. I had to remind myself that the kids were just playing, Sparky wasn't in any danger. In fact, me being an overprotective mama wisp was why the kid even knew what rabies were. I should probably cut back on the safety-first bedtime stories.

Ceff stood and leaned against a row of filing cabinets, but kept an eye on Sparky. Even Forneus was smiling at the kid. I had to force myself not to get distracted.

"Then we're in agreement," I said, nodding at Jinx. "Gaius was angrier than he should have been."

"That would suggest that Sir Gaius felt threatened by what transpired with the stealing of these corpses," Ceff said.

He remained leaning against our filing cabinets, arms crossed over his muscular chest, but I noticed the small shift in his posture. Ceff took a step to widen his stance and he shifted his weight to the balls of his bare feet, adopting a fighting pose. I wasn't even sure he was aware of it, but Jinx definitely noticed.

She raised an eyebrow, but I shrugged, looking away. We were all on edge and would probably continue to be until we solved this damn case.

"Do you think it mattered that whoever stole the bodies did it using necromancy?" I asked, leaning back in my chair. I stared at the ceiling, trying to sort through what we knew of the case so far. "Like, would using magic to raise the dead be any more of an insult or threat to Gaius than just digging them up and driving away with them?

"In this case, I believe that the means is less important than the resultant theft," Forneus said, nodding slowly. "The property to which Sir Gaius stakes his claim, in this case the property being corpses buried within the city's boundary lines, was most certainly the focus of the contract he so unceremoniously dropped on your floor. While concerning for us, I do not believe the vampire's ire is much affected by the raising of the dead, only the theft of their corpses."

"Anyone else concerned that bodies buried within the city limits belong to the vamps?" I asked. "I, for one, am not cool with this."

"Seconded," Ceff said, managing to play rabid doggy with Sparky and Humphrey while we went over the case and a possible threat to our city. Our lives were so weird.

"Me three," Jinx said.

"No threeee!" Sparky yelled, pulling himself onto two feet, tiny hands on his hips.

We'd gone over the dangers of saying something, especially a promise, three times. In the world of faeries and demons, a thrice told thing could ensnare and bind. Ceff flashed me a worried look, but it disappeared behind a jovial mask as he asked Sparky how to count to ten. Toddler distracted and crisis averted, but yes, I might need to cut back on teaching my kid about everything that was scary and dangerous. In our world, that was a hell of a lot.

I might not have been as relaxed lately as I'd thought.

"What about the fact that the stolen bodies were fae, rather than human?" I asked, returning to our original problem.

I'd worry about how to improve my parenting skills later. The fact that I'd been more prepared to fight monsters than to become a parent probably had something to do with why I was screwing up. I never planned for this. I had no idea what I was doing.

Thankfully, that didn't keep the kid, or Ceff, from loving me. Ceff carried Sparky over and shot me a questioning look. I nodded and opened my arms, and Ceff dropped the toddler into my lap. Sparky babbled happily for a second and fell fast asleep.

My breath hitched and a silly grin slid across my face. Somehow, in the midst of the worst danger and horrors, I'd become this little guy's safe place. I was more shocked than anyone.

Sparky sucked on the end of one of his long, floppy ears and I shifted him in my lap. I didn't mind getting visions from my kid, most of his memories were happy and the ones that weren't featured me as his hero, but a vision would cut into time that I didn't currently have.

"So, why is Gaius so mad?" Jinx asked.

"A new player in town?" I asked. "Someone stupid enough or powerful enough not to care about his harvesting rights?"

"It is a possibility," Forneus said. "That would surely cause Sir Gaius to feel threatened. Though to what purpose it's still unclear. Without that knowledge it is hard to say if they are a threat only to Gaius, the vampires, or to us all."

I knew that Kaye's current state of health and the glaistig's recent disappearance—both of which I was largely responsible for—created a power vacuum. It was inevitable that, eventually, someone or something would come to fill that void. It was that pesky balance thing again.

But I hadn't stood idly by waiting for the next power player to roll into town. Remember those security measures that I'd mentioned? They included spreading rumors and misinformation. And I'd had help from the best gossipmonger our city had.

Torn cast rumors into the shadows, whispered to his cats, and into the ears of our enemies. As far as the world knew, Kaye O'Shay was here in Harborsmouth, making preparations to build a new Emporium bigger and better than before. More importantly, we gave the impression that she was out for blood, pissed off by the Wild Hunt's attack, and itching to flex her magic might in the protection of her city.

It was, of course, mostly a lie, and fae aren't supposed to be able to tell a lie. But that's what made the exaggerations and half-truths so believable. Even our enemies could be fooled when the misinformation came from the truth-telling, shadow-dwelling cat sidhe. Who better to know Harborsmouth's secrets? And who better to believe than a faerie who cannot tell a lie?

It had worked, so far. It probably helped that we already had other major players in our midst. Loathe as I was to admit it, Sir Gaius and his nest of vampires kept a lot of nasties away. Not many supernaturals are brave enough or dumb enough to enter a vampire's territory uninvited.

"We need more information," Ceff said.

I had a prime source for the city's secrets. Too bad that source had taken to prowling the city's less savory bars and bringing every faerie he met into his bed.

It wasn't the casual sex that squicked me out, not really. It was the fact that Torn, Lord of the Cat Sidhe, leveraged sex for information. He was proud of the secrets he stole during what he called "pillow talk" and that niggled at my concept of consent.

Whether it was wrong or not, it was damn sneaky. For all his help with the disinformation campaign, I'd avoided Torn lately, which might be unfair. But his relentless flirting with Jinx, who was now betrothed and sick to death of Torn's innuendos, and his prowling of Harborsmouth's underbelly had put a strain on our relationship.

We'd been though a lot together, but every time I accepted him as part of our family, he did something to piss me off. Jinx said it was part of a self-destructive pattern that I, of all people, should understand.

I avoided Jinx's statement, but I couldn't stay away from Torn. Deep down, I knew that he was hurting. My father, one of Torn's few friends, had returned to Harborsmouth only to turn around and leave again. That loss left a hole in my heart. What had Willem's leaving done to Torn?

I imagine all the wedding talk hadn't done much to soften the blow. Everyone was pairing off, leaving Torn on his own. I used to think he preferred it that way, but I used to believe that about myself too and look at how that turned out.

Huh, maybe Jinx had a point. Torn and I might be more alike than I thought.

"I know a good place to start, I said. "I need to visit Torn."

CHAPTER 7

I left Jinx and Forneus to hold down the office. Humphrey agreed to stand sentinel and guard the building from the rooftop. Ceff promised to take Sparky to visit Marvin and Hob, and to quietly ask questions and let the local fae know about the zombie problem. Since that problem only involved gerbil-like creatures, I hadn't contacted the local Hunters' Guild, yet.

That was why, with drizzle soaking into the neck of my jacket, I scowled at the end of the alley that served as the entrance to the cat sidhe court. The alley ran alongside Club Nexus, a nightclub that served as a hidden haunt for Harborsmouth's paranormal underworld. The ogre manning the door at Club Nexus nodded, but he didn't make eye contact.

Funny how the not-so-secret-secret of my royal lineage had made its rounds, and the various ways that members of the local supernatural community had reacted. Some had declared fealty, some demanded a duel, but most just seemed extra awkward around me. Being a faerie princess isn't all it's cracked up to be. It was like high school but with more homework.

That homework, researching in Father Michael's library and reading what I could from any of the salvageable books from the scorched wreckage of The Emporium, was one of the reasons that Torn was such a conundrum.

Dragons? Centaurs? Demons? Unicorns? There were entire libraries of information. But try to look into the workings of the cat sidhe court and you hit a wall of shadow and obfuscation. Not that I was surprised. I expected nothing less from my friend. And, yes, for all his lesser qualities, Torn was, to my eternal surprise, a friend—a fact I should probably remind him of now that his guards were staring me down.

"Let her pass," Torn said. "The princess is an ally, for now."

"I think we can agree that we're not only allies, but, hopefully, also friends," I said, stepping into the alley.

Torn's eyes widened and I flashed him a bemused grin and a shrug.

"I know, it surprises me too," I said. "But you know I'm telling you the truth."

I could rarely tell a lie these days, and only the tiniest white lies at that. Visiting Faerie had changed me. Or rather, it had hastened my body's transformation to its true form, burning away the spell that had kept me mostly human. But I'd never been human, at least not biologically. I was the offspring of a wisp king and the queen of the Unseelie court. That came with new truths with massive ramifications. It also meant I was becoming sensitive to cold iron and I couldn't tell a lie, mostly.

"What truth is that, princess?" he asked, raising a hand to one of his scarred ears as if he hadn't heard my admission.

"We are friends," I said with sigh.

I ran a gloved hand through my hair. Of course, Torn would drag this out. Cat's really do love toying with their prey. Mab's bloody bones. He was enjoying himself.

"Can you repeat that?" he asked with feigned innocence. "I didn't quite catch..."

I threw a wooden stake from my utility belt and hit him on the shoulder. He was lucky it wasn't one of my blades. A cat hissed, but Torn tipped back his head and laughed.

"Ah, princess," he said. "You do keep things interesting. What can I do for you, my friend."

I was going to kill Torn.

"I need your ears," I said.

He flicked his scarred, battle-worn ears, setting the dangling bones and fetishes to clattering, and I sighed.

"Not your ears, the ears of your cats, your spies," I said, rolling my eyes. "I need to know if they hear anything about grave robbing, or of any reanimated dead."

"Vampires? Ghouls?" he asked. "You need to be more specific, princess."

I sighed, nearly growling in frustration.

"Zombies."

"Zombies?" he asked, eyes shining with interest. "Someone is robbing graves and creating zombies?"

"Yes, well, ah, of a kind," I stammered.

"A kind," he said.

"A type," I said through gritted teeth.

"What type of zombies are we talking about?" he asked. "It's not Halloween. People would be talking if human corpses were shuffling down Congress Street."

"Zombie gerbils," I muttered. "Well, they're really faeries, but that's a long story."

Torn leaned in close, and I immediately regretted this visit and my decision to ask the cat sidhe for help.

"Oh, I'll make time for that story," he said, licking his lips. "I thought the shadows held the best whispers, but you win, princess. Zombie gerbils. This I've got to hear."

"Since you seem so enamored with the critters, you want to help me hunt them down?" I asked.

A Cheshire cat grin slid across Torn's scarred face and he flexed his hands, claws sliding in and out of my fingertips.

"I thought you'd never ask."

CHAPTER 8

I frowned, squinting into the mist and fog surrounding the pet cemetery. How the heck had I ended up here, hunting zombie gerbils with Torn? I was wet, my head ached, and the tendrils of fog swirling and slithering around my ankles gave the vertiginous impression that there was no solid ground beneath my feet.

"You know, I meant to ask if you or your cats have heard of any new supernaturals in town," I said, scanning the cemetery walls for the best place to enter. We certainly weren't strolling through the iron gates. "Gaius is pretty pissed off that someone is stealing his corpses."

"And you're none too happy that someone is raising zombies," Torn said. I jerked my head in his direction—did Torn's spies have eyes and ears in my office—but he shrugged. "What? It's not like I don't know you, princess. You're a hero. You protect the city. It's what you do."

So, why did he sound so damn depressed about it? Torn usually liked the fact that danger followed me around.

"You didn't answer my question," I said.

"Noticed that, did you?" he asked. "You've been spending too much time around your fish man."

"He's not a fish man," I said. "Ceff is a kelpie. He shapeshifts into a horse, not a fish."

A horse with gills and who can breath underwater, but that was beside the point.

"If it smells like a fish and swims like a fish..." he muttered.

"Torn, for the love of Mab, answer the question or shut up," I said.

He lifted a clawed hand and mimed zipping his lips, locking them, and throwing away the key. Sure, he was a friend. He could also be a total jerk. I'd have to approach the questions from a different angle, just like entering the damn cemetery.

I frowned and stomped over to where the iron fencing disappeared into a thick tangle of shrubbery.

"This way," I said.

I waved us forward and strode down a side street without glancing over my shoulder to see if Torn followed. He would or he wouldn't. I wasn't here to herd cats. I was here to catch and dispose of a bunch of zombie gerbils and get to the bottom of what was really going on here in my city.

I'm supposed to protect Harborsmouth and keep innocent civilians safe from supernatural threats. It's my job. I'd survived so many paranormal baddies, odds were good I'd survive this too. Maybe, if I told myself that enough times, I'd believe it.

I squinted into the thickening fog, scanning the area for threats. I didn't like how the rain had turned to drizzle, followed by a mist, and now a dense, impenetrable wall of fog.

"Think this fog is natural?" I asked, not surprised when Torn answered.

"It's possible," he said.

"But not probable," I said.

"When is anything ever normal or natural when you're involved?" he asked, wiggling his eyebrows.

I winced. Torn was right. I'm sure he meant it as a compliment, but things in my life were rarely simple. I glanced up and down the narrow street, but there wasn't a soul in sight.

I paced away from the stone wall and tilted my head back. I let a small amount of my wisp magic leak through my mental barriers, just enough to allow my eyes and skin to glow faintly. While I despised Gaius' nickname of "corpse candle" wisps really could light the way.

It's where some of the fairy tales about wisps leading men to their doom comes from. Not that I'd lead anyone to their death. Oh no, not me. Sadly, that was less convincing as I stood outside a cemetery with a danger loving, thrill-seeking cat sidhe at my side. Torn better hope he had nine lives the way tragedy followed me around. Even the ever-present mist evoked the moors where my ancestors are said to have led men to their watery graves.

Not so long ago, I lacked the knowledge and control needed to prevent my eyes and skin from glowing. That was before I'd found the key my father, Will-o'-the-Wisp, had left for me, sending me on a quest to find and open a hidden door to Faerie. I'd made it to my father's court. Heck, I'd made it to my mother's court too. That scared the jeepers out of me.

But it wasn't in Mab's ice palace that I'd learned how to control my powers. No, that feat required the wisp court and the torturous training set by my uncle. Thoughts of Kade and his ultimate betrayal made me want to burn the world to the ground. Ironically, it was his tutelage that gave me the ability to control those urges. Fate has a twisted sense of humor.

I directed my wisp magic outward and the glow illuminated the wall that rose from the sidewalk here, driving the shadows into the cemetery beyond. My brow wrinkled as I studied the situation and weighed our options.

There was a gap here in the iron scrollwork and pointy fencing that topped most of the wall, almost like someone had left us a back door. I just hoped it wasn't a trap.

"Need a hand, princess?" Torn asked, threading his hands together.

I shook my head, bouncing on my toes.

"I've got this," I said.

I took a deep breath, rolled my shoulders back, and ran. What I reached the base of the wall, I leapt. I didn't make it fully over the wall, but I did manage to drive my gloved fingers into a handhold, my boots kicking until they caught a narrow crevice. I ungracefully pulled and kicked my way to the top of the wall.

Torn crouched at the top, lips twitching in a grin.

"Go ahead and laugh," I said, rolling my eyes. "We all know cats are the better climbers."

"Oh, no," he said. "Wouldn't think of it."

A wheezing purr poured out of him and he wiped at his face.

"What now?" I asked. "I couldn't have looked that ridiculous."

"You did, actually," he said. "But that's not what I was laughing at. It's just...you can fly, princess."

Oops. He had a point.

"Whatever," I said with a shrug, ignoring his sniffs as he regained his composure. "Then what would I do with my jacket? I can't fight with my hands full and I'm not leaving it down on the street."

"You do have a point," he said.

He was no longer laughing, so I turned my attention to the pet cemetery below. The headstones and graves were smaller than their human counterparts, but the place was no less oppressive. I lowered my voice to a reverent whisper as my eyes examined the scene.

"Do you think it's a coincidence that the corpses that were stolen are faeries?" I asked. "And why are faeries buried in a pet cemetery?"

In all the hubbub earlier, I'd forgotten to ask Ceff about that. I considered calling him, but shook my head. I'd give Torn a chance to answer first.

"I doubt it's a coincidence," he said.

"Should I be worried that faeries were buried in a pet cemetery?" I asked, eyeing the iron gates warily.

"The roads to Faerie are closed, princess," Torn said. "What did you think we did with our dead?"

I jerked my head up, eyes wide.

"You mean, we bury our dead here?" I asked.

"Some of us do," he said.

A look flashed across his face, of anger or sadness or frustration, it was hard to tell. We'd all suffered losses in recent months. Torn and the cat sidhe for all their talk of neutrality had fought alongside us against multiple foes, including the Wild Hunt.

Then what he said sunk in. Torn and his people took the form of cats. He ruled over the city's actual cats too, but that's not what we were talking about. We were talking about faeries being buried where the humans buried their pets.

My stomach twisted.

"I'm sorry," I said. "I wish it wasn't like this. I wish...I wish that my evil bio mom hadn't abandoned her throne and locked you and your people out of Faerie. I wish there was still a way for you to return to Faerie to honor your dead."

His eyes widened, but he looked away with a quick nod.

"We should examine the scene of the crime," he said, leaping down to land on his feet.

I frowned, measured the distance to the nearest headstone, and jumped. I didn't land on my feet, but I also managed to not break my neck. I'd take that as a win.

Torn was probably right about me using my wings to fly. Not that I'd tell him that. His ego didn't need a boost. Plus, I wasn't even sure that I could trigger the transformation that would make my wings emerge right now, not after so carelessly drawing on the ley lines during my dustup with Gaius.

My jaw still hurt from gritting my teeth so hard, I'm surprised they hadn't cracked. Tapping into ley lines was stupid, but I'd do it again in a second. Nobody was laying a finger on my best friend. Not even zombie gerbils.

Something small scurried to my left, managing to lurch and skitter all at the same time.

"Found one," I said, wrinkling my nose. "Unless it's an injured sewer rat."

With a flick of each wrist, my throwing knives hit my palms. I widened my stance and took a slow, cautious step forward. I didn't think a bite would give me a hankering for brains, but I sure didn't want to know what kind of visions I'd get from an animated corpse.

"That's no rat, princess," Torn said.

"Good," I said, circling the headstone where I'd lost sight of the zombie. "That's good, right? We came looking for zombie critters. Now we just need to, um, take care of them."

Taking care of them involved some stabbing, some pouncing, and a hell of a lot of cursing.

"Sweet Titania," Torn swore with an angry, yowling hiss as he shifted back onto two legs.

"I hope that was the last of them," I said, frowning at the plastic grocery bag where we'd been storing the bodies.

The zombies were in various states of decomposition. Even worse, we'd taken to cutting off their heads, just in case, and the sound of tiny, furry heads rolling around inside the plastic bag was making my stomach churn.

Torn spit out a desiccated rodent that smelled like rotten meat, and hissed.

"Come hunt zombies she said, it'll be fun she said," he muttered, spitting and coughing up a hairball.

"I never said to eat them," I said.

"I didn't eat them," he said. "I caught them in my teeth. How else do you expect a cat to catch a rodent?"

He had a point. If it hadn't been for Torn's ability to shapeshift into a cat, I don't think we would have caught them all. The tiny zombies weren't particularly smart, but they could go in places I couldn't fit. There are a surprising number of hidey holes in a cemetery.

"You did good," I said. "The corpses match the corresponding number of empty graves. That should be the last one."

"Until our mystery friend comes along and raises more," Torn said.

"I've been thinking about that," I said, carefully wiping my blades on a patch of grass. "Why target faerie corpses? It must have been intentional. Whoever did this didn't touch any of the normal rodents buried here, and there's plenty of gerbils and hamsters in this place. Even a chinchilla or two."

"And we're careful to bury our dead beside theirs," he said. "Our lives are long, but memories fade. Better not to rely on a glamour that must be maintained."

"I noticed that," I said. "I guess I expected your dead to all be in one place apart from the pets and under a glamour or a don't-look-here spell. But that makes sense. Someone would have to come along and recharge a spell like that. This way, there's less likelihood of being discovered."

That couldn't be easy. How many cat sidhe had Torn personally buried here, laying their bodies beside the pets of strangers. I didn't envy him that task or the pragmatism of such a decision.

"So, whoever did this had to have been targeting faeries," I said. "But why?"

"Residual magic would be my guess, princess," he said.

"Care to clarify that?" I asked.

Sometimes, it was like he was speaking a different language.

"Just like the land of Faerie itself, faeries are made of magic," Torn said. "When we die, some magic stays behind, like a residue. Think of our corpses like a vessel, but with just a few drops of magic."

"Like batteries," I said. "Are we really talking about corpse batteries?"

"It's an apt analogy," he said.

"And you think this necromancer is stealing faeries to harness their magic energy," I said.

"It's possible," he said.

A jolt of panic zipped through me.

"Think they'll target the living next?" I asked.

Living fae must contain more magic than the lifeless shell left behind, right?

"I don't think so, princess," he said, turning in a slow circle. "Whoever did this used necromancy. That kind of death magic has little control over the living. They'll stick to the dead, unless the living get in their way."

"But you said their magic has little control over living," I said.

"That doesn't mean they can't hurt us," he said. "They'd just send their zombie minions to kill us. Then we'd be fair game."

I shuddered. No way was I letting some necromancer kill innocent people and turn them into murder puppets. That was gross and all kinds of wrong.

"We need to warn our friends and allies," I said. "This might get messy, and dangerous. Imagine if this necromancer raises something bigger next time."

"Sounds fun," he said, leaning forward, eyes wide and unblinking.

Yep, that wasn't creepy or anything.

"There could be panic amongst the humans," I said. "We can't cover up zombies if they start shambling down Congress Street. Like you said before, that kind of thing tends to get noticed. The secret of our existence could be threatened."

"Not so fun," he said, shoulders slumping as if deflated. A serious expression flit across Torn's scarred face. "I survived the Burning Times by the skin of my teeth. There was no skill or elegance to those kills. All that existed then was pain, torture, and blood."

"Blood," I said, hitting the palm of my left hand with my fist. "That's it!"

"Did you hit your head, princess?" he asked. "Breathe in too much corpse gas? I told you to hold your breath while decapitating the zombies."

"I'm not loopy or high on corpse gasses," I said. "Also, ew."

"Then what?" he asked. "You don't usually get excited over blood."

"I do when it might lead us to our necromancer," I said. I grinned showing too many teeth. "Remember the Leanansidhe?"

"How could I forget?" he asked. "You and Jenna had all the fun."

"The Leanansidhe used necromancy to try to raise her dead lover, what was left of him anyway," I said, wrinkling my nose.

I still had nightmares of Leanansidhe dancing with her lover's skeleton. It was beyond creepy, almost as creepy as her redcap minions.

"And she fueled her magic with blood," he said. "Blood and bone and sacrifice."

"And rituals," I said. "Necromancers perform blood rites to raise the dead."

"Where there's a blood ritual…" he said.

"There's evidence," I said.

I nodded, but Torn still looked unconvinced. It didn't do much to reassure my already faltering confidence.

"Something is still bothering me though," I said. "We're assuming that this necromancer wants faerie corpses for their magic residue. But if that was the intent, why weren't the zombies summoned back to the necromancer."

"Leaving them to scamper around the cemetery does seem like a waste of magic," he said.

I frowned. If I never saw another fluffy, zombified adorable rodent again it would be too soon.

"So, we have a plan," I said. "We keep an eye out for any bloody magic circles, sacrificed goats, that kind of thing."

"And if more zombies turn up, we follow them back to their maker," he said.

Oh, goody. That sounded like tons of fun.

CHAPTER 9

When they depict private investigators on television, they never show the endless, tedious boredom of waiting for something to happen. I hadn't sat still since our zombie hunt in the pet cemetery, but a search for blood ritual sites had turned up a big heap of nothing.

Torn became so bored, he muttered something about watching paint dry and sulked in a shadowed corner of our office.

It was possible that the necromancer had moved on. That would be great for the city, less so for me. I'd promised Gaius that I would get to the bottom of his corpse thief problem and my faerie blood was holding me to that bargain. My head pounded and I yawned so wide that my jaw snapped.

"You should get some sleep," Jinx said, bending down to pick up a pen that had rolled off my desk.

"I don't think that's possible," I said, rubbing a gloved hand over my face.

Our office swam before me and I shook my head. If I feel asleep, I wasn't sure if I'd be able to wake up again. I needed a lead in this case. There had to be something I was missing.

"Jinx is right," Torn said, pulling away from the wall with feline grace. "Get some rest. We can renew the hunt tonight."

The bell above the door jingled and my head snapped up, but it wasn't Ceff. He'd called and said he'd keep asking around at Eden Park, the magic garden where so many fae had recently relocated. He had Sparky with him, and they'd be safe in the garden with Marvin and Hob and my pooka allies. But that didn't lessen the disappointment when Benmore walked through the door.

"What's the dwarf doing here?" Torn asked.

I sighed and slumped in my chair.

"Probably has some message from Gaius about his freaking harvesting rights," Jinx said, rolling her eyes. "I'll go see what he wants."

She stood and schooled her face into a bland smile, but Benmore froze.

"I see you are holding court, m'lady," Benmore said, managing to scurry away while bowing so low his beard collected dust bunnies.

Jinx might be unfailingly polite, it was why she was the outward facing half of our partnership, but I was less so. I failed at politeness most of the time. I frowned and palmed my knives.

"I don't think he means you're busy hanging out with your friends," Torn said, raising a scarred eyebrow.

I nodded and growled with frustration. There was more to the dwarven mayor's words. I didn't like the implication that I was lording my royal rank above my friends or, even worse, making them demonstrate their fealty by bending a knee. Even if, from his perspective, my human vassal was on her hands and knees in front me.

Oberon's eyes, my life was complicated.

"Benmore, stay," I said, raising a gloved hand.

He flinched, beard twitching. Great, there was an unintentional ring of command in my voice that was sure to make this situation worse. Benmore removed his bowler hat and fiddled with his pocket watch. Oh, yeah. I'd definitely made things worse, my behavior only supporting the dwarf's assumptions about me. He looked ready to either kneel or run.

"I do not wish to disturb you amidst your duties," he said, frowning. At least, I think he frowned. It was hard to tell with dwarves due to their copious facial hair, but I'd spent enough time around the gnomes, thanks to Gwenda, to decipher certain beard movements. "But I will do as you command."

The dwarf wasn't the only one frowning.

"I wouldn't... I didn't mean...argh!" I growled. "Please, don't bow. We're all friends here."

It was a bit of a stretch to claim friendship, since Benmore and I weren't all that close, but the remnants of my father's curse and my strange upbringing allowed the white lie to pass my lips.

Torn looked amused, but Jinx swept over with a chair and a dish of honey candies.

"Here we are, Mr. Benmore," she said. "Now how can we help you today."

The dwarf eyed the chair warily, but settled into it at the sight of candy.

"Sir Gaius wants an update on Miss Granger's progress," he said, pocketing a handful of sweets. "Our master is quite distressed and demands a swift conclusion to the case."

Gaius wasn't my master, but I let the comment slide, for now.

"We're doing everything we can to pursue the matter and find whoever is stealing from Gaius," I said. "Unless you're here with information that can help us solve the case, I'm going to have to ask you to refrain from visits that will only waste my time and yours."

Look at me adulting with the big words. I hadn't even stabbed anyone, yet.

"I'll show you out, Mr. Benmore," Jinx said, getting up to stand at his shoulder.

We'd shown the necessary hospitality. Now if only he'd kindly get the hell out of our office before my head exploded. I reached for a bottle of aspirin and Benmore frowned, but he finally stood and followed Jinx to the door.

"Gaius must be taking this personal if he's sending his henchmen to check on you so soon," Torn said.

I nodded, swallowing the bitter tablets and washing them down with holy water. It's not as weird as it sounds. We had a priest bless our water cooler once a week, providing us with a steady supply of holy water. If Gaius had been standing near my desk when he'd threatened Jinx, he'd have received a nasty surprise. Sadly, the water cooler had been out of reach. I made a mental note to move the dispenser closer to Jinx's desk, and the bell above the door jangled again and Torn slid into the shadows with a wink.

What now?

But it wasn't another one of Gaius' minions. It wasn't my fiancé either. Standing in our waiting area was a young Asian woman in her late twenties or early thirties, wearing a raincoat and holding a small dog to her chest. She stroked the dog with short, quick motions, bouncing him in her arms.

It was going to be a long day.

CHAPTER 10

T he woman standing in our office waiting room was
obviously agitated. Good thing my best friend had years of
experience with helping someone calm down. Getting hit with
visions and seeing through glamour had made my life hell as a
kid. By the time Jinx came into my life, I was a teen with a
phobia or three. She was great at trauma triage and, unlike
me, people usually didn't run screaming when she smiled.

"What a cutie," Jinx said, smiling and shifting the focus
to the woman's dog. "What's his name? Is he a mini
Schnauzer?"

"Her name is Angie," the woman replied automatically.
"She's a Schnoodle, um, a Schnauzer-Poodle mix."

"Think she'd like some water?" Jinx offered. "Or a cup of
tea for you? It's no trouble."

"Oh, um, no thank you," she said. "Well, maybe the tea.
For me, not Angie."

"Honey or sugar?" Jinx asked, pouring two cups from
the carafe atop the squat filing cabinet closest to her desk.

"No, thank you," she said.

I waited for Jinx to complete the ritual of hospitality. It
wasn't an actual magic ritual, but the results tended toward
the miraculous. It's amazing what a kind word and a cup of tea
can do. I'd seen her do the same with fae folk with fangs and
claws who didn't speak a word of any human language I
recognized. Kindness was universal.

But if this woman was turning down honey, my money
was on her being human. That and she looked totally normal
with my second sight. Even her dog was just a dog, albeit a
particularly adorable one with a breed name that sounded like
a type of sugar cookie.

Jinx brought over the cup of tea and a jar of dog biscuits
and set them beside the chair facing my desk. With a curt nod,
the woman settled in the chair, dog on her lap. She took a
fortifying sip of tea, the cup clattering against the saucer due to
shaking hands. I watched her brace herself, but she lifted her

chin, and met my eyes. I had a bad feeling that I didn't want to hear whatever thing it was that made coming to me such an ordeal.

"What can I do for you, miss...?" I asked.

She looked from me to Jinx, who stood nearby, ready to jump in when we were ready to draw up a contract, or if I started scaring the client.

"Brandy," she said, absently stroking her dog. The dog looked at me suspiciously and showed its teeth, and I avoided making eye contact with it. Some animals can see through glamour or at least sense our otherness, and this dog and its owner were already on edge. "Brandy Palmer. And I don't know if you can help. It's just that I didn't know where else to go, who else to tell, but I have to tell someone and I remembered your ad in the paper about taking on weird cases, no matter how strange, and that you're a psychic, you know, like, different. And I thought, I can tell her. She won't think I'm crazy. She'll know what to do."

Brandy spoke rapidly, all the while bouncing the dog on her knee. While I had no idea what she'd seen, it was obvious that I needed to handle this carefully.

"It sounds like you came to the right place," I said soothingly, keeping my voice gentle.

Brandy laughed, a touch of rising hysteria in her voice.

"Now that I'm here, I'm not so sure," she said. "I guess I expected beaded curtains and crystal balls."

"Sorry, The Emporium has that covered," I said.

I winced inwardly. Madam Kaye's Magic Emporium had the cheesy psychic kitsch market cornered, at least it had until I'd caused it to burn to the ground. I didn't seek out havoc, but danger and destruction had a bad habit of finding me.

I had a feeling this visit was more than a simple case. Hopefully, whatever had scared this woman wasn't something of my own making.

"You said you needed to tell us something?" Jinx asked.

"You probably won't believe me," Brandy said, shaking her head. "I don't believe it and I was there."

My eyes flicked to Jinx. That sounded like our kind of case, all right.

"You made the right decision, Brandy," Jinx said. "You can tell us. No judgement, I promise."

"Jinx is right," I said. "You can talk to us and it's in, um, confidence. Trust me, I've seen things that can't be explained. I get it if you're scared."

I was going with my gut here, but something had this woman spooked and we needed her to feel like she could tell us whatever it was.

"You won't believe me," she said.

But she'd slumped in her chair and her words were less certain.

"Try us," I said. "You'd be surprised what I believe these days."

"We're discreet," Jinx said, pouring more tea into Brandy's cup. "Detective-client privilege and all that."

Brandy sighed.

"I was walking Angie down by the pier, near where the carnival used to be," she said. "You know where I mean?"

I nodded, a sinking feeling in the pit of my stomach.

"At first, I thought it was a bunch of kids in Halloween costumes or people filming a movie," she said.

"Because?" Jinx asked.

"Because they were zombies dressed like clowns," she said. "Or clowns dressed like zombies. Zombie clowns."

Brandy started to laugh, and a chill ran up my spine.

"Can you describe these clowns?" I asked. "You said 'at first' you thought they were actors. What changed your mind? What made you think they weren't part of a movie or TV shoot?"

Harborsmouth wasn't a huge city, but we did attract the occasional film crew. Actors dressed as zombie clowns, or clown zombies, was plausible.

"Oh, I thought I said," she said, looking back and forth between us. "It was the smell."

"The smell?" Jinx asked.

"Yes, they smelled like spoiled meat," she said, looking a bit green.

"And they were dressed like clowns, you're sure?" I asked.

"Heck, yes," she said. "Quite sure. Top quality costumes too. I really thought they must be filming a movie, but a film crew doesn't record smell, do they?"

Her eyes were wide and glassy. She was in shock.

I reached into a desk drawer and grabbed another dish of honey candies. I slid them across the desk, waving for Brandy to help herself. Jinx raised an eyebrow, but I shrugged. Brandy may not have a faerie's sweet tooth, but the sugar would help the shock.

There wasn't much more I could do. It's not like I could admit to the existence of zombies or tell Brandy about the carnival fae. And our local vampire lord, although technically an ally, was in no condition to erase this woman's memory, even if I'd been in a position to ask him for a favor, which I certainly was not.

"Oh, that was my friend's punk band!" Jinx exclaimed.

"A band?" Brandy asked, blinking.

"Sure!" Jinx said. "They look totally scary, right? And they smell horrible."

Jinx wrinkled her nose exaggeratedly. It would have been funny if she wasn't saving our butts by selling a lie that just might preserve our secret existence.

"Well, yes, but..." Brandy stuttered.

"It's their image," Jinx said. "And, you know, the hamburgers they left in their van. Now their costumes smell terrible. Totally rank. I heard one nightclub wouldn't even let them on stage."

"It was just a...punk band?" Brandy asked.

Humans are innately prone to disbelieving the weird and uncanny. Give them a reasonable, scientific explanation and they'll usually take the bait. Nobody wants to believe that monsters roam the streets. I should know. I'd started seeing the monsters beneath their magic glamour when I was just a kid. If there'd been a way to turn off my second sight and tell myself it was a hallucination, or a punk band, I would have done it in a heartbeat.

Blinking and clutching her dog, Brandy followed Jinx to the door. It was a pretty magnificent performance, and nobody got hurt. When the door closed, Jinx flipped the closed sign and dropped into the vacated chair across from my desk.

"Thank you," I said.

"No problem," she said. "She was nice. No reason for her to have nightmares. It was the least I could do."

"It's a good thing my partner is so brilliant," I said.

"Hella brilliant," she said.

"Okay, hella brilliant," I said with a snort.

I smiled, but it didn't last.

"Think the necromancer is squatting in the glaistig's old territory?" Jinx asked.

"Sounds like it," I said, letting out a heavy sigh.

Until recently, the carnival fae had lived on the pier where the glaistig, known to her subjects as the Green Lady, ran a combination amusement park and freak show that was actually a cover for the more monstrous faeries who were incapable of glamour. Due to my inability to control my wisp powers or create a glamour to cover up my otherness, I'd almost ended up one of them, swearing fealty to the Green Lady.

In the end, I'd found another way to solve my glamour problem. But the glaistig and I had history. We'd butted heads, and I'd made bargains with her, more than once. That might not have ended too badly, but the Green Lady had been impatient, a common trait of the long-lived, and tried using Jinx as a bargaining chip. She'd forced my hand, but I won't lie. I enjoyed knocking the glaistig down a notch and rescuing an enslaved incubus and succubus in the process. I didn't like bullies.

Admittedly, we did more damage than was necessary to save Jinx. The Green Lady's tent burned and some of the adjoining grounds were damaged, but the carnival fae were unharmed. I thought that I'd sent a clear message not to mess with me and mine. I figured that once the dust and ash settled, we'd start over on more equal footing. I never thought the glaistig would leave in the night, taking all of the carnival fae with her. One day they were there, a bit scorched but alive and operational, and the next the amusement park was shut down and abandoned.

Until now.

CHAPTER 11

Torn finally emerged from the shadows of my office, where he'd eavesdropped on our client's visit, and we decided to continue tour zombie hunt. Jinx hadn't been thrilled to be left behind, but it was still during business hours. Plus, Brandy may not be the only human to see zombies on our city streets. We had to keep the doors of Private Eye open, just in case.

That left me once again with the cat sidhe lord.

"As much as I'm enjoying this team-up, I think it's time for reinforcements," I said, texting Ceff with our location and a quick update on the current zombie situation.

It wouldn't take Ceff long to get here, even with a pitstop to drop Sparky off with Jinx back at the office. Torn and I were on the jogging trail that ran along the harbor, halfway between Private Eye and the abandoned amusement park sprouting up from the pier like a riot of poisonous mushrooms on a felled tree stump. Rising from the clusters of faded and ragged circus tents stood the Ferris wheel, the distant rusty creak of its cars mixing with the cry of seagulls.

"You think I can't handle more zombies?" Torn asked. "You wound me, princess."

"I think we can use another set of eyes on this, especially from someone with sway with the local water fae," I said. "Ceff isn't just king of the kelpies. He's one of the most powerful water fae leaders in these waters. The selkies, merfolk, and merrow are all either allies or have sworn allegiance to him."

"I suppose that could be useful," he said. "Maybe. It's not like I'm on the best terms with the merfolk right at the moment."

"Yeah, that tends to happen when you don't bother to call a girl back," I said. "I thought you were all wise and immortal, Torn. Sleeping your way through the entire mermaid clan was stupid, even for you."

"The two are not synonymous you know, wisdom and immortality," he said. "Not that I'm admitting to any wrongdoing. Merfolk culture is supportive of polyamory."

"And I'm not saying it isn't," I said. "Look, I know I have my hang-ups, but I don't have a problem with sex between consenting adults. I also don't have a problem with you taking on multiple partners. What I do have a problem with is you not being honest and upfront about your intentions with any of your partners. Also, not a fan of how you gather some of the merfolk's secrets. It's sneaky as hell."

"Why thank you," he said.

"Wasn't a compliment," I said. "But I think you know that already. You've been on a self-destructive downward spiral ever since my dad left. I get it. It sucks. And I can hard relate. I miss him like crazy. But he's gone, and I'd rather not lose you too."

"You almost sound like you care, princess," he said.

"That's because she loves you, silly cat," Ceff said, pulling himself out of the harbor and up onto the jogging and cycling trail where Torn stood dumbstruck. Ceff let out an equine snort and flashed Torn an amused grin. "What? Somebody had to say it. You two were never going to."

Ceff shook himself dry, like a horse shedding water from its coat. From one second to the next, he went from swimming in the harbor to bone dry. No water pooled around his bare feet. Even his low-slung jeans were dry. It was a neat trick.

Torn might be rooted to the sidewalk, but I had no such problem. I took a step toward Ceff, need swirling within me. My betrothed held still, reading my intent, as I leaned in for an embrace. It was all restraint and anticipation and the promise of what ifs. We didn't have time for a vision right now, but, so long as we didn't touch skin to skin, I'd be fine.

No crippling visions. No getting hurt. No fear.

I'd come a long way. Ceff had been a big part of that, but in his own weird, annoying way, so had Torn. There were times when Torn was like holding a mirror. I didn't want to be alone forever. I loved my new family and, sure, family can hurt you, but that's because they're worth the pain and sacrifice. Even Torn.

"Fine," I said with a shrug. "Ceff is right. I care. But how about instead of standing around talking about our feelings, we go search for some dead people."

"Oh, thank Titania," Torn said.

"This way," I said.

It didn't take us long to reach our destination. Becoming fae had its downsides, what with the iron allergy and the assassins, but a wisp, a cat sidhe, and a kelpie can sure travel fast when we put our minds to it. Being on a jogging trail also gave us the advantage of not needing to worry about attracting undue attention. If we moved a bit too fast, or a tad more gracefully than a human was capable, that was surely due to the fading light and dancing reflections off the harbor.

I waved my friends over to an overgrown shrub and a wall of chain link fencing that rose from crumbling pavement, sand-filled potholes, and patches of untrimmed grass. We had a clear view of the carnival's service entrance.

Too bad we were also downwind of an extremely ripe garbage dumpster.

"Why are we here?" Torn asked, showing his teeth in disgust.

Torn had lurked in the shadows of my office, listening to every word our client had said about the zombie clowns she'd seen while walking her dog near the carnival's front entrance. Armed with that info and our past adventures together, Torn probably assumed I'd go storm the front gates, fireballs blazing. He was forgetting that I wasn't just a wisp princess with magic powers, or a woman who attracted destruction like a minotaur in a china shop. I was a private investigator, and a damn good one.

Being a P.I. had taught me a lot, including the importance of recon and surveillance. We needed to follow the clues and gather more intel. There would be time for blades and fireballs later.

"Because there aren't many places to bury a body within the Green Lady's territory," I said.

"Former territory," Torn said.

"Sure, whatever," I said. "The point is, if those zombie clowns that Brandy saw were the animated corpses of carnival fae, they had to come from somewhere."

"And the most likely place was within the carnival grounds," Ceff.

"Yeppers," I said. "I think we can all agree that, for good or ill, there are some faeries who can't be buried within the city's human graveyards or pet cemeteries."

"And the sea refuses those she does not deem worthy," Ceff said.

I'd worried about death plenty, but I never thought much about what happened after. About the arrangements that the survivors were left to make. Cremation, becoming worm food, or burial at sea had all seemed like trivial details when we were fighting for our lives. But Ceff's words rang with the importance of such a decision.

That was probably a conversation that Ceff and I needed to have. Until now, I hadn't bothered to research water fae funeral rights and customs. I fidgeted with the straps of the wrist sheaths that held my blades and licked my lips. I kind of sucked at this betrothal thing.

"But why here, at this odiferous loading dock," Torn asked. "Why not stroll through the front gates?"

"That would be foolhardy," Ceff said. "And dangerous."

"Exactly," Torn said, licking his lips.

"We're not strolling through the front gates without doing some recon first, so we know exactly what we're facing," I said.

"I suppose we could use the element of surprise," Torn said, bouncing on his toes and eyeing the service entrance. "Pouncing from the shadows is fun too."

"The element of surprise and the possibility of danger aside, I think this is our best bet for finding where the carnival fae buried their dead," I said. "Think about it. Most of the carnival grounds are on top of the pier, sitting above water. There's very little actual land for burying corpses."

"Please tell me we're not here to go dumpster diving," Torn said. "I may hold court in an alley, but our trashcans are filled only with delicious kibble, not rotting corpses."

I eyed the flies buzzing around the overflowing dumpster and frowned. Could it be filled with decomposing bodies? Now that was a cheery thought.

"Do you believe their dead could be discarded in that dumpster?" Ceff asked.

"Only one way to find out," I said.

CHAPTER 12

"I'll let you do the honors, fish breath," Torn said, gesturing toward the putrescent, malodorous dumpster.

"And how did you come to the conclusion that I should receive such an...honor?" Ceff asked, voice dripping with derision.

"Eeny, meeny, miny, moe totally should have caught a cat sidhe by the toe," I said, nodding knowingly at Torn.

While I was relieved that they weren't insisting that I be the one to touch the dumpster, it seemed unfair not to at least draw straws or something. Torn was just being spiteful.

"Wouldn't you like to try, princess?" he said, waggling his foot.

I mock shuddered. It didn't take much effort since touching his toe would probably drag me down in the psychic muck and mire to drown in centuries of visions of Torn's exploits.

Deep down, I knew we were all just stalling. Nobody wanted to get up close and personal with a pile of reeking garbage. It was obvious that no deliveries or garbage pickups had occurred since the glaistig's departure. That was plenty of time for refuse to become a fetid pool of nasty inside of a dumpster.

There were also the flies and maggots to consider. I didn't think they'd give me visions, but they were certainly disgusting. Too bad the back lot of the carnival was our best option for getting answers.

"Rock, paper, scissors?" I asked.

"No," Ceff said. "Not this time. We are in a hurry and it is just a receptacle for waste, after all. Ready?"

"Okay, sure," I said, taking a step back and raising an arm across my face.

Ceff flung the lid of the dumpster back and blanched. Even Torn shook his head and hissed. Great. Just swell.

I stepped forward and lifted myself up on tiptoes, immediately regretting the clear view. I made it a few seconds before I lurched toward the chain link fence. I wanted to run.

I hadn't really expected a dumpster filled with body parts. I'd been a naïve fool.

"Is that...are those?" I asked, unable to finish the question.

Some things just shouldn't be said out loud. Too bad Torn didn't have such reservations.

"If you were going to say a jig-saw puzzle of rotting body parts from various carnival fae, then yes, princess," Torn said. "That's exactly what that is."

I swallowed bile and took small, shallow breaths.

"Not helping," I said, tamping down the urge to be sick.

I lifted myself up onto the balls of my feet and took another look inside the dumpster. This time, I tried to pretend the dead people were movie props or Halloween decorations. My brain wasn't totally convinced, but it helped enough for me to take a visual inventory.

"There's at least a dozen people in there, probably more," I said, breathing shallowly through my mouth.

"Maybe the Green Lady ran out of burial space?" Torn asked. He stepped back and rolled his eyes. "What? It's a legitimate question. We know their territory didn't include a lot of land for burials, and I never heard of the carnival fae burning their dead."

"This is not a burial," Ceff said, horror written in the planes of his face. "This is sacrifice."

"Like, as in blood rituals?" I asked.

"Perhaps," he said, nodding. "Though what could bring a leader to do this to their own people is beyond my comprehension."

"Perhaps, fish breath?" Torn asked, a scornful smirk tugging at his scarred face. "I'd say the chances of these faeries being part of a blood sacrifice is a pretty sure thing, what with the complete absence of blood, like, anywhere."

He swaggered over to the dumpster, gesturing smugly at the clue we'd missed. I'm sure we would have noticed eventually, when I was less busy trying to pretend the body parts were from inanimate mannequins instead of from formerly living, breathing faeries. But Torn had a point.

"They were exsanguinated," I said, shaking my head. "But how? I don't see any bite marks."

"Which rules out vampires," Torn said. "I know. Unless you want to go in there and examine each piece, I'd say the top layer is a good enough sample to theorize we're not dealing with vampires."

Was it wrong that I was searching for puncture wounds, hoping that these were vampire kills? Vampires were strong and deadly, but I knew how to kill them. An unknown threat was much scarier. Better the enemy you know.

"Their throats were slit," Ceff said, voice low and weary. He drew his trident and used it to gently move what was left of a faerie's arm, tilting it for a better look. "Wrists too."

"Definitely sacrificed then," I said, studying the scene.

"If this is where they stuffed the sacrifices, what's left of them anyway, where's the blood-soaked magic circle?" Torn asked, tilting his head to the side, pondering the question like it wasn't all kinds of wrong covered in wrong sauce. "And where's the vessel?"

"Vessel?" I asked. It was the only part of this conversation my brain didn't shy away from.

Unless he was talking about blood vessels. I really hoped he wasn't still talking about blood.

"Like the batteries we talked about, princess," Torn said. "Normally, I'd expect slaughtered goats, a necromancer's bloody magic circle, and a virgin or some artifact or reliquary for the magic to be contained within."

"We've got more than slaughtered goats," I said, frowning.

"But no vessels," Torn said.

"So, the question remains, where did the magic go?" Ceff asked.

My knee jerk reaction was to make a "remains" joke, but I was too busy swatting flies and trying to keep my stomach contents on the inside.

"I don't know," I said, absently. "But these were people, faeries, like us. Should we say something? A prayer?"

Ceff bowed his head, looking more tired than when I'd first saved him from the each uisge. He'd survived captivity and enslavement, his immortal body carrying the marks from those iron chains forever. But that had been his own suffering.

This was the loss and desecration of loyal subjects whose leader had left them behind.

If Ceff needed a moment, I'd grant it to him. Torn, however, was less reticent.

"It's no use, princess," Torn said.

"They are gone," Ceff said, nodding in agreement. It was rare for these two to agree on anything, but this was no time to celebrate, not while presented with a dumpster filled with body parts. "The part of them you call people, what you think of as a soul, is gone, returned to Faerie."

"And the residual magic?" I asked.

"Stolen by a necromancer," Torn said. "Do we get to go and kill him now?"

"First, we have to find out where this necromancer is," I said.

"How do you propose we do that?" he asked.

I stared at the dead bodies, forcing myself to see them as faeries, as people. If any of my family was in there, I'd do what needed to be done. If any piece of my friends were in that horrific pile, I would reach out and touch them. There would be no hesitation. I would seek out a vision and I would do whatever it takes to find the person who killed them and desecrated their bodies.

My friends weren't in that dumpster, thank Mab. And although I did hesitate, I knew what I needed to do. I was a hero, after all.

"The worst way imaginable," I said.

"Are you going to read their entrails?" he asked.

Scratch that, the second worst way imaginable. Leave it to Torn to think of something even worse than being pulled into a vision by the victim of a blood sacrifice.

"No, I'm going to touch something belonging to one of the victims and try to find a lead in this case," I said.

"I will watch your back," Ceff said, looking at me intently.

"Pull me out if it gets bad?" I asked, ignoring how small and weak my voice was.

"I have seen Jinx do this for you many times," he said. "I know what to do."

I nodded, giving him a brittle smile. I was a hero. I had to do this, but I didn't have to like it.

I took a deep breath, immediately regretting it due to the pervasive stench of rotting meat. I grimaced and dug around in my jacket pockets for the sports mouthguard I kept for times like these. I might choke on it, especially if I barfed, but that was preferable to biting off my own tongue. With a quick, practiced motion, I shoved the mouthguard over my front teeth and rolled my shoulders, trying to rid myself of some of the tension there.

Next, I closed my eyes and said a prayer that this wouldn't go goblin fruit-shaped. Visions are tricky at best, an eternal nightmare prison at worst. Probably better not to dwell on the horrific possibilities and get this over with.

I tugged off my leather gloves and shoved them into my jacket pockets. I sure as heck wasn't setting them anywhere near that dumpster. That would be like putting vipers in your own armor. I tried not to flinch as fetid air touched my naked hands. I cocked my head, looking for the least disgusting thing to touch. Not an easy choice under the circumstances.

I reached for the most innocuous item, a discarded shoe. It wasn't a clown shoe, thank Mab. It was a simple, ruby red slipper with no heel and one elasticized strap across the arch, similar to a ballet shoe.

My fingers rested on the shoe and I stiffened, every muscle in my body going rigid. The world spun upside down. That wasn't unusual for a vision, but this one left me teetering on a razor-wire high above a crowd of gaping humans—directly over a tank of shark-like creatures with too many teeth.

Mab's bloody bones. Of course, I had to go and pick an item belonging to a tightrope walker. Oh, and here come the throwing knives and flaming hoops. Great. Just great.

But while I wasn't thrilled about the situation, the faerie whose vision I was riding was totally loving it. She was completely in her element, thriving under the spotlight.

Actually, that might be a little too accurate. It was a good memory, sure, but the faerie really was receiving sustenance from the bright light. It was some kind of ultraviolet lamp, granting her, us, the extra power to perform a flawless high-wire routine.

If I'd had any doubt about that logic, it was banished when I caught sight of our leg as we wrapped it behind our neck with ease, hopping gracefully along the wire on one foot.

That leg was covered with bark, and when a strand of our hair slipped in front of my face, it was tipped with small, green, heart-shaped leaves that rustled as I spun in a perfect pirouette.

I could have watched the dryad's hair for hours. Too bad my psychometry had other ideas.

If I thought the heights, shark creatures, and deadly flames were scary, I was sadly mistaken. That had been a happy memory for the faerie, a proud moment of accomplishment in service to the Green Lady. What came next was more than terrifying. It was downright disturbing.

Knowing the glaistig's feudal-like rule over the carnival fae, I expected that if I caught sight of the dryad's killer, the blade that bled her would be held by a cloven-hooved woman cloaked in green. I hadn't been prepared for the spinning gateway of swirling blue light or the horrifying creature who stepped out of it.

The monster wasn't quite a vampire or a zombie, although his hands were skeletal and his face little more than a corpse. I didn't know who or what he was.

What I did know was that the creature was powerful. He wore black robes and a silver crown, and magic radiated off him like decomposing uranium.

His fingerbones danced and twisted with strange, arcane gestures and where they slid through the air magic skittered. Beneath our feet the dead stirred, responding to the necromancer's power.

His voice, like the bastard offspring of a death rattle and a rattlesnake, slithered through the circle, whispering in the dryad's ears even as he slashed her wrists to drip-drip-drip onto the ground.

"Flesh and bone."

"Bone and blood."

"Blood and ash."

"Let it be done."

He slashed with blade and bone. Death came swiftly. At least that was one mercy. The faerie never experienced the necromancer's full depravity or the disarticulation of her body. I only caught flashes of those foul deeds as I clawed myself to the surface, struggling to escape a sea of hot, coppery blood, gasping for air.

I spit out my mouthpiece, ran for a tangle of weeds at the edge of the parking lot, and barfed up my breakfast. It was mostly coffee, thank Mab.

I strode back to Ceff and Torn, running a hand through hair damp with sweat. Crap, I was still bare-handed. I hastily pulled on my gloves and took a shaky breath.

"Are you well?" Ceff asked.

The dryad's ruby red shoe was nowhere in sight, for which I was grateful.

"Mmm hmm," I said. "Never better."

"We going to kill something now?" Torn asked. "I'm feeling the need to stab something."

"You and me both," I said. "But there's one more place we need to search."

Torn sighed and rolled his eyes.

"And where would that be, princess?"

"The carnival fae's graveyard," I said, nodding toward the maintenance building. "Over there. On the other side of this building."

"Perhaps, we should all rest for a moment," Ceff said, the skin around his eyes tight with worry.

"No," I said, glaring at him.

I played a good game, but I couldn't hide my feelings from Ceff. He knew what a vision like the one I'd just had cost me. He also knew enough about bargains to know that I was beginning to feel the side-effects of headache and fatigue. Projectile vomiting and holding my head like it was going to fall off were probably also dead giveaways that I wasn't at my best.

Screw my best. We weren't just dealing with zombies—which, for the record, was bad enough—we were dealing with a necromancer who didn't hesitate to murder, bleed, and dismember innocent people. So, I stared down my betrothed, daring him to tell me what I couldn't do, all the while knowing that his suggestion to rest was the same advice that I would give him under the circumstances.

A sound like a combination of someone dragging something heavy and drunken footsteps interrupted the silence. I held my breath, eyes going wide. Ceff's trident was suddenly in his hand, fully extended, and Torn flexed his claws. While I knew they were both formidable in a fight, I wasn't ready to reveal our presence here. Not yet. We needed more information about the necromancer and his bloody rituals. I had a feeling we'd get those answers if only we could examine the nearby graveyard, preferably uninterrupted by shambling zombies.

I glanced around, looking for cover. The only place to hide was either inside of or behind the dumpster. It wasn't a difficult choice. We were stuck between a rock and an extremely disgusting, nightmare vision inducing, stinky place.

I dove behind the dumpster.

"I hate you," I muttered, scowling at Torn who managed to hide in a much less odiferous shadow.

"You're the one who wanted to skulk around and collect evidence," he whispered. "If we'd stormed the front gates, we wouldn't be in this mess."

"No, we'd be dead," I said.

"Like I said," he said.

A zombie clown ambled around a large, rusty fuel tank, heading our way. It wasn't really a clown, but it hurt my brain less than trying to formulate a more accurate description of the monstrous looking faerie. I'm sure that in the dim lighting of a circus tent, and with less deterioration of the makeup painted on its face, it would have passed for a clown. Human imagination and a subconscious ostrich-like sense of self-preservation would have filled in the rest of the illusion.

"I suggest we stop talking now," Ceff said.

The zombie didn't come straight at us, thank Mab. At the corner of the building, it turned, following a weed-strewn gravel path. With its back now to us, and the immediate threat gone, I edged out from our hiding spot.

Torn was faster. With the litheness of a tiger, he sauntered the alley that ran alongside the building, turned back, flexed his claws, and winked.

I shrugged. I was a psychic detective. Somedays you follow the money. Other days you follow the dead.

CHAPTER 13

"Come on," I whispered, waving us forward.

Torn cocked an eyebrow, but I shook my head and gestured with two fingers, pointing back and forth between my eyes and the alley the zombie clown was shuffling past. This would be eyes only. I wish there was a gesture for please don't get us all killed or keep your weapons in your pants, Torn. That would come in handy.

At least the cat sidhe lord was stealthy. I'd give him that.

Torn prowled forward, taking the lead. I didn't mind him taking point on this. He was best equipped for stalking the zombie clown. I might have the potential light-footedness and dexterity of a faerie, but I was still new to my abilities. The faster reflexes and dancer-like grace had lain dormant in blood and bone for years due to my father's spell. Torn was much more practiced at hunting prey and being sneaky.

Ceff was also gifted with faerie grace and the benefit of centuries of practice, moving along with fluid elegance. But rather than rush forward like a wave breaking on the shore, Ceff preferred to follow at my heels, providing a solid defense in case we were attacked from behind. Not that he couldn't provide a powerful offense. He just preferred to support those he loved, and surprise, surprise, that included me. He would always have my back.

So, with Torn in the lead, Ceff bringing up the rear, and me as the wisp in the middle, we followed the zombie clown as it shuffled along weed and sawdust strewn paths between outbuildings. It wasn't terribly exciting. It was just us, a zombie wearing ridiculous footwear, and the creak of the Ferris wheel looming over everything like a rusting sword of Damocles.

But as the outbuildings gave way to canvas tents, I started spying the occasional zombie rodent, even a zombie bird that walked along rather pathetically, no longer able to fly. The zombies were heading in the same direction as our clown. It wasn't what I'd call a horde, but it was disconcerting, nonetheless.

I rubbed at my neck, fidgeting enough to catch Torn's attention.

"Ants in your pants, princess?" he asked, leering at my jeans.

I rolled my eyes, but Torn did have a point. My skin itched, burning needles of pain stinging my face and arms, even the soles of my feet.

"Anyone else feel like they're being licked by a pixie?" I asked.

Torn, for once, actually looked concerned. His face had gone ashen, body losing its feline grace as it went rigid. Oh, sure. He was all eager to go storm the gates and go fight an uber powerful necromancer, but mention the mere possibility of being pixed and the man was shaking in his supple leather boots.

"I do think zombie pixies are where I draw the line, princess" he said, eyes darting around warily.

"There do not appear to be pixies, or any of their hives, in the vicinity," Ceff said, studying me. "But you are reacting to something."

"Maybe, I'm allergic to zombies?" I asked.

As far as allergies went, that wasn't too bad. I mean, some people had to give up peanut butter. I just had to stop a necromancer and his pet zombies.

I wonder if there was a cream for that. Zombiedryl? Necrosporin? I should call Arachne. She might know. Normally, I'd ask Kaye, but she was stuck in a coma. My eyes watered and I blinked rapidly. Pesky allergies.

"It is more likely that you are reacting to an influx of magic here," Ceff said. "Something about this place feels wrong somehow."

"Now that you mention it, fish breath," Torn said. "There's nothing alive here, except us. No seagulls. No raccoons. Not even any grass or weeds growing here."

He was right. The carnival grounds should have attracted scavengers. But the only things moving around these tents were dead. We'd left everything living back at the outbuildings.

"Think this itchy death magic stuff might kill us?" I asked.

Ceff shrugged, but Torn looked ready to dance a jig. Weirdo.

"I suggest we gather whatever information we can and leave this place," Ceff said.

I nodded. He didn't have to tell me twice. I felt like I had a case of poison ivy and, with Marvin's nickname for me, I was fully aware of the irony. The sooner we found out where the zombie clown was headed, the sooner we could fall back and regroup, and maybe take a bath in calamine lotion.

Torn stalked forward, increasing our pace. We made it past two larger tents, nearing the center of the carnival grounds, when he raised a hand, bringing us to an abrupt halt. He waved around the corner and I frowned.

Ceff and I inched forward, edging around the tent for a better look at whatever had caught Torn's interest. I gasped.

Zombies of every shape and size followed the paths here. Some even tore or gnawed through canvas in their urgency, tripping over tent pegs and tangling in the guide ropes. Zombified centaurs, gryphons, goblins, and leprechauns converged on the sprawling black and red building that crouched at the edge of the courtyard like a spider.

The building was painted to look like the walls oozed blood, the faces of tortured ghosts pressing against the black paint. A track ran in and out of the building, rusty metal seats with safety bars sitting as silent witnesses to the zombies lurching their way inside. The fact that the opening was painted to look like the bloody maw of some fanged beast made it even more disturbing, if that was even possible.

"You have got to be kidding me," I muttered.

There were dozens of the zombie faeries. Maybe more. If those zombies were heading home to their master, then that meant he was hiding inside the creepiest place in the entire abandoned carnival grounds.

Death magic tingled along my skin and I shook my head. Mab's bloody bones. The necromancer was hiding out in the Haunted House.

CHAPTER 14

I've been told that I'm stubborn. I've been called a fool. But every cell in my body was telling me that now was not the time to fight. With the ever-growing horde of zombies heading toward the carnival Haunted House ride, I spun on my heel and ran.

I guess I'd learned a thing or two in recent months. Surviving more than one supernatural invasion will do that. My calves burned, but I put on a boost of speed, sprinting to the alley where we'd first caught sight of the zombie clown.

I'd been worried about that one zombie. Funny how things change. I took a ragged breath and rubbed a gloved hand over my face. At least my skin had stopped itching.

"What now?" Torn asked.

"We still need to search the graveyard," I said. "That's where they performed the blood ritual in my vision."

"Isn't that where that zombie clown came from?" he asked.

I spun, jumping at shadows. I palmed my knives, feeling the weight of spying eyes.

"Are you okay?" Ceff asked. "I still think we should take a rest before continuing our investigations.

"Please say we're going to hunt zombies now," Torn said. "I'm getting bored with hide and seek."

I scanned the rooftops and glanced up and down the alley, but there was nothing there. Maybe, Ceff was right. I probably did need a break after that vision and after the fear of chasing after a zombie clown and running from a nightmare-filled Haunted House had drained my body of adrenaline. I was tired and twitchy, but I didn't have time to rest.

"Yes, no," I said, catching my breath. "Yes, I'm okay. No, we're not hunting zombies right now. That was some hardcore magic back there, fueled by a whole lot of blood and death. I'm not eager to go toe to toe with our necromancer just yet."

"Speak for yourself, princess," Torn said.

"Don't get me wrong," I said, smiling and showing too many teeth. The afterimage of a ruby red slipper was still etched into my mind alongside the knowledge of what had happened to those carnival fae in the dumpster and what was happening to the bodies of faeries in cemeteries all over Harborsmouth. "I want to take this evil bastard down."

"And you must complete your contract with Gaius," Ceff said. "Faerie has a way of holding us to our promises."

Sadly, I knew that all too well. I'd made more than one bargain since becoming increasingly fae. Headaches and exhaustion were just the tip of the iceberg. If I didn't find out who was encroaching on the vampire master's harvesting rights, I could wind up dead.

"Think telling him it's a necromancer who's hiding out in the carnival grounds would do the trick?" I asked, half-heartedly.

"No," Ceff said shaking his head. "Gaius was aware of the zombies from the beginning, so we can assume he knew a necromancer was the most likely suspect. The only new information you have to give him is a possible location."

"And then he might show up in a rage, throw a major temper tantrum, and cause this whole thing to go sideways, fast," I said.

I shivered, remembering how quickly Gaius vamped out in my office, fangs as big as a damn walrus, pink-tinged spittle at the corners of his mouth. The vampire master most definitely had zero chill about someone stealing his corpses. Finding a Haunted House ride filled with his rightful property, as he'd see it, frolicking under his nose would surely piss him off.

"Not to mention steal all the fun," Torn said.

"Yeah, that's totally what I was worried about," I said, letting out an amused snort. "Come on. Break time is over. Let's go check out that graveyard. It's not far."

Ceff gave me a concerned glance, but nodded. If I looked as bad as I felt, I'm sure I was a sight to behold. I probably didn't look all that different from some of those zombies. I was tired, I might still have vomit on my face, and I'd been skulking around dumpsters.

And that was before we went to investigate the Green Lady's burial grounds.

I walked around the maintenance building, listening for the telltale shuffle of zombie feet, but it was strangely silent. It was as if the world held its collective breath as we stepped into the weed-strewn graveyard.

"This place is creepy," I said.

As if the yawning graves, splintered coffins, and broken headstones weren't bad enough, there were the seemingly random things the zombies had left behind. The bits and pieces of corpses, left like leprotic breadcrumbs, were disgusting. The shoes, framed photographs, and teddy bears were downright disturbing.

"And empty," Torn said. "Looks like our clown friend was one of the last to dig its way out and join the others on their pilgrimage."

"There should be more," Ceff said.

A chill ran along my back and neck like spiders skittering up and down my spine.

"What do you mean?" I asked. "More what?"

"More graves," he said, frowning. "The carnival fae were numerous and they lived a dangerous life here under the Green Lady's rule. There should be more graves. A lot more."

"Awesome," I muttered. "Just awesome."

"Maybe they took them somewhere else to bury?" Torn asked.

Ceff shrugged, but his brow was wrinkled. I wasn't great at math, but now that I thought about it, Ceff was right. Something hinky was going on.

"I could touch one of the mementos their loved ones left here," I said, forcing my shoulders back, holding my chin high. "Grief usually leaves behind a psychic impression. It might give us a clue as to why there aren't more graves."

I waited for Ceff to argue. A small voice in the back of my mind even wanted him to. But he nodded and gave me a reassuring smile. Even Torn was being supportive in his own way.

"How about that photograph, princess?" he asked, pointing at a framed photo of a centaur and his family. "Probably less likely to scramble your brain than a child's toy."

"Thanks," I said drily.

The vision wasn't easy, but Torn was right. It didn't scramble my brain. I did, however, wind up face down in grave dirt.

I spit and frantically wiped at my face. My gloves were back on my hands, thank Mab. Ceff must have slid them on while trying to pull me back to myself. That explained the sensation of being shot from a catapult into a stone wall.

Every muscle in my body ached, but I was alive, and I had learned something valuable.

"I know where the other bodies are," I said.

"Where?" Torn asked, leaning forward.

"Some place called the Necropolis," I said.

"Cheery name, has a nice ring to it," he said.

"Right, well, I guess the Green Lady made a deal for her dead to be buried there," I said. I swallowed and pulled myself to my feet. My legs felt like soggy gluten-free noodles, but I was upright. "I think they ran out of room here."

I waved a gloved hand at the small graveyard. Ceff nodded.

"Not enough land here," he said. "And the vampires wouldn't have been willing to sell any of their precious real estate."

"And burying carnival fae in the human or pet cemeteries around the city would have risked breaking the First Law," Torn said. "The glaistig already walked a fine line with her carnival freak shows. The courts would not have shown her or her people mercy."

"It gets better," I said. "This Necropolis? I'm pretty sure it's whatever was beyond that portal from my vision."

"Looks like we need to learn more about this Necropolis," Torn said.

"I agree," I said. "I also need a change of clothes."

"You do smell, princess," he said.

"Thanks," I said, rolling my eyes. "I need to stop by the loft. I can grab a change of clothes and check in with Jinx before heading to Father Michael's."

"I don't like churches," Torn said with a frown. "Count me out."

"I was hoping you'd say that," I said. Torn shot me a suspicious scowl, and I lifted my hands. "Someone needs to stay here and keep watch."

Unless they were crossing saltwater, or could swim, the zombies weren't leaving the abandoned amusement park. Once they entered, they didn't exit out through the front gates. If so, we would have seen them.

"I think we can agree there's only one way in or out," I said. "And every zombie we've seen was heading toward the Haunted House ride. There's no other way off this pier that doesn't involve saltwater, not unless they have an invisible boat."

Saltwater nullifies most magic. I was guessing that a dip in the harbor would have dire consequences for the necromancer's pets. It was enough to have me wishing I owned a small island somewhere. Actually, it wasn't a bad idea for a honeymoon destination.

"They don't have an invisible boat, do they, fish breath?" Torn asked.

It was a valid question. My second sight can cut through glamour, but there are other types of spells that can hide and obfuscate. Torn should know.

"No boat," Ceff said with a wry grin.

"So, there's probably a portal inside the Haunted House ride, like the one I saw the necromancer use in my vision," I said.

At least, I hoped so. Sort of. It was better than imagining a clown car situation. A zombie clown car situation. I covered a rising giggle with a cough. If I started laughing now, I wouldn't be able to stop.

I bit my lip and focused on the pieces of fur and bone dangling from Torn's tattered ear. It reminded me of how death clung to me and my friends, and how much the cat lord enjoyed, reveled in, that fact.

"The portal that leads to this Necropolis?" Torn asked.

"Maybe," I said. "I need to get more information to know for sure. But whoever stays here and keeps watch will have to be a skilled fighter. And brave. It might be dangerous. Maybe even deadly."

"I'll do it," Torn said.

CHAPTER 15

With Torn working surveillance and with an idea of where the city's zombies were heading, I could breathe a little easier. Too bad I smelled like death and rot and the juice usually reserved for the bottom of a garbage bag. The sickeningly sweet stench was so putrid I could barely stand it, but here on the outskirts of the harbor, we weren't all that far from Eden Park, the magic gardens that were now home to many of the city's less violent faeries.

"Let's pay Marvin and Hob a visit," I said, a fluttery feeling in my chest as I set off down the sidewalk.

"They were safe when I visited with them this morning," Ceff said.

I knew that Ceff had paid our friends a visit, Sparky in tow, informing Hob and Marvin of a potential zombie threat. The threat at the time had been zombie gerbils, but still, they'd had a warning that there were new supernatural hijinks afoot in Harborsmouth and that Gaius had worked himself into a dusty lather over it.

"I'd still feel better checking in with them," I said, lifting a shoulder. "And it's not like I can call them with an update."

Not anymore. The words hung in the air unspoken.

The gardens of Eden Park were beautiful and nothing less than an Oberon damn miracle. The gorgeous greenery, clean water, and riot of flowers sprung from the bodies of the fallen huntsmen. Many of the more peaceful and diminutive faeries now thrived here in what once had been nothing more than broken pavement, rusty corrugated warehouses, and a small stream choked with sewage and contaminated by industrial waste.

These gardens were the silver lining in a thundercloud. Hob had relocated here after the disaster at The Emporium. He now lived in a hearth within a small gnome cottage which was the abode of his lady love, Gilda. I knew he missed his old home, but I wasn't so sure how he felt about Kaye. She'd betrayed all of us after the magic I inadvertently gave her twisted the kind woman we'd come to love. Hob had ignored my offers to take him to go visit Kaye at the asylum. The situation was complicated.

I pushed more speed into my stride, worry winning over fatigue. I couldn't let anything bad happen to Hob. He'd already been through so much. In fact, so had Marvin.

Marvin had also moved to Eden Park, but his motivations were as clear as the water that now ran beneath his bridge. The young troll cared for Hob and was worried about the grouchy, old hearth brownie. So, Marvin had moved here too.

At least it made visiting easy. Or so I thought as I stepped across a remaining patch of broken pavement and froze, one booted foot inches above the mossy green path into Eden Park. Marvin, Hob, and the gnomes weren't the only faeries that I'd helped relocated to these gardens. I'd also invited the pookas to move out of the treehouse in my human parents' yard and into a swanky club house here.

It was a decision I regretted as I stared down the length of a spear. Which wasn't all that long really, due to it being a sharpened pencil, but the tip was needle-sharp and pointed at my eyeball. The fact that it was held by an orgy-loving pooka who hovered at chest level made the situation even more troubling. Even if he didn't poke my eye out, I might be wishing he had when the visions kicked in.

I struggled not to twitch or shiver, allowing myself only to slowly raise my hands in surrender. Yep, that's me, the hero of Harborsmouth, surrendering to a pooka. To a human, it would look like I was terrified of a pigeon or a flying squirrel. Good thing the magic of this place kept humans from wandering in. Of course, I had no idea if those magics would protect the faeries who lived here against their zombified dead.

Maybe, I should be thankful the pooka was patrolling the perimeter. Or maybe I'd die with a pencil lodged in my brain. Either way, I was about to find out.

"I surrender, Violet," I said. My voice barely shook. Go me. "Can I come in?"

Violet wasn't his real name, but none of the pooka had been forthcoming with their real names. There's power in a name, and the tiny faeries weren't keen on handing that power over to a big person, even if I was an honored ally and former friend to their fallen leader. I'd actually been teasing when I first started calling them by the colors of the glow-in-the-dark condoms they wore on their heads like hats. But they seemed to like the nicknames and so the names had stuck and I'd had to get really creative with synonyms for primary colors.

Violet scowled at me for an entire second before nodding and lifting his pencil spear to rest against his shoulder. I heard a sharp intake of breath and shot a glance over my shoulder where Amber was using Ceff's neck to pole dance while simultaneously threatening him with a dagger made from a sliver of glass. You can say what you want about pookas, but they sure can multitask.

"Hey, Amber," I said. "Nice moves. Think you could take that dagger away from my betrothed's jugular now?"

That caught the pooka woman's attention.

"His neck can juggle?" she asked, flinching away from Ceff and eyeing the pulse in his neck suspiciously. "You big people are weird."

She had been doing an acrobatic strip tease around my fiancé's neck while threatening to decapitate him, but we're the weird ones. That made perfect sense.

I heard a familiar giggle and spun around. It wasn't more pookas, thank Mab. There on the mossy path stood Marvin snickering and wiping at his eyes. Hob was bent over beside him wheezing and slapping his knee.

"Hey, kiddo," I said, waving at Marvin.

I squinted, belatedly realizing that he had donned some kind of makeshift armor. It actually made him pretty intimidating. Somehow, he'd gone from shy teenager and grown into a young man without me noticing. That was actually kind of worrisome since I was a detective. Noticing things is what I do.

"Hiya, Poison Ivy," he said, scraping his fingers noisily against his jawline, and the stubble growing there, pretending to itch.

It was an old joke, but I laughed anyway, blinking a bit at his five o'clock shadow. Seriously. When had he grown up?

"Ye should ha seen ye face, lass!" Hob said, dancing a little jig.

"Har har," I muttered.

"It was less amusing than you might think," Ceff said with a pained expression.

I snorted and turned to the pooka guards now marching back and forth across the path.

"So, it's okay for us to enter?" I asked, pointing at my chest and hooking a thumb over my shoulder. "Both of us? Me and Ceff?"

It was best to be clear when dealing with a pooka.

"None shall pass!" Violet bellowed.

Amber giggled and started spinning in circles.

"What if my name is None?" I asked. "His too."

"Oh, then go right ahead, Miss Granger," Violet said.

I strode onto the spongy, moss-covered path and followed Marvin to the nearby bridge he called home. We'd have some semblance of privacy there alongside the babbling brook and less risk of anyone using my betrothed's neck as a dance pole.

"So," I said, gingerly taking a seat on an overturned log. "No sign of zombies?"

Marvin didn't sit, instead leaning his bulk against the side of the stone bridge that spanned the crystal-clear water. His gaze never straying long from the pathway leading back to the park's entrance, one of his large hands mere inches from a club that look suspiciously like a twin to the tree I now sat on. I was relieved to see his vigilance, but also a little sad. I knew what it was like to have to grow up too fast.

"They wouldna' dare," Hob said, his bushy, caterpillar-like eyebrows lowered in a scowl. "But if they do, Marvin will crush their wee skulls."

He smacked his hands together, the clap making me jump.

"About that," I said, wincing. "We've got more than zombie gerbils now."

"Zom-bie cats?" Marvin asked.

"Um, bigger," I said. "Actually, there might be cats too, but I'm more worried about the zombie clowns and centaurs and gryphons we saw over on the pier."

If there were cats in that zombie horde, I hoped I never saw them. I'd seen enough nightmare fodder.

"Tankerabogus," Hob said.

"What a the what now?" I asked.

"The Green Lady's clowns," Ceff said, shaking his head. "I should have realized it before, but tankerabogus are rare. I did not realize there were any near Harborsmouth."

Until now, I'd only thought of those zombies as clowns. It was easier that way. But I was sorry to hear that a rare type of faerie had died here and I'd never even had the opportunity to meet them.

"They were hunted relentlessly during the Burning Times due to their habit of kidnapping and eating small children," Ceff said.

Okay, maybe not so sorry. It was probably a good thing they were dead, undead, whatever. If I'd known about their appetites for innocent children, I might have killed them myself.

"Only the wee naughty ones," Hob said.

I shot the hearth brownie an incredulous look and he fell over backward, giggles coming from behind the rock he'd been perched on.

"What we do?" Marvin asked.

"I need you both to stay here and help guard the gardens," I said. "These are your homes and there's a lot of helpless faeries living here. Ceff and I need to go take care of some things, so we can't stay here and protect the others. Can I count on you?"

"Mm hmm," Hob mumbled in the affirmative from behind his rock.

I wasn't sure, but he might have been stuck. Not that I was worried. Hearth brownies were much more agile than they looked. He'd be fine once he stopped giggling.

Marvin, on the other hand, wasn't laughing. In fact, he looked deadly serious.

"I will protect," Marvin said.

CHAPTER 16

"**I** need a shower," I muttered.

"You, girl, need all of the showers," Jinx said. "You smell like death, you're covered in dirt and grease, and is that vomit in your hair?"

I shuddered. Usually, having psychometry and being touch phobic gets me out of pawing through garbage and sifting through grave dirt. When we found a zombie clown shuffling around the carnival grounds, I hadn't expected to see an entire horde of zombies filing into the Haunted House ride. To say the sight was disturbing was an understatement.

And that was the least disturbing thing we'd found. The dumpster filled with exsanguinated body parts would haunt my dreams forever.

"It's been a long day," I said, peeling off my leather jacket and hanging it on the coatrack beside the door. I didn't normally let that jacket out of my sight, but nothing about today was normal, and my jacket smelled horrible. I didn't want to bring it into my bedroom, which was where I was headed when Jinx stepped in front of me.

"Here," she said, shoving a paper cup filled with hot coffee.

I raised an eyebrow, but took the cup.

"What, are all the mugs dirty?" I asked.

"No," she said, eyes raking over me from head to toe. "You are."

I shrugged. She had a point. Jinx sniffed and sashayed back toward the kitchen which smelled even better than my coffee. I'm pretty sure me reeking of garbage and dead things was ruining dinner.

"Be right back," I said, heading toward the bathroom. "Thanks for the coffee."

When I reemerged, I was fully transformed, wearing the blissfully clean jeans and long-sleeved sweater that Jinx had snuck into the bathroom for me. Have I mentioned how awesome my best friend is?

"You're awesome," I said, discarding the mental filter I usually hid behind.

Like I said, it had been a long day and it was far from over.

"Right back atcha," she said, using a spatula to slide a pile of eggs and bacon onto my plate.

I started salivating like a barghest. When was the last time I ate? I didn't have time to do the math, too intent on keeping my balance as a demon toddler tried his best to knock me over.

"Ivyyy!" Sparky squealed.

Oberon's eyes, the kid was cute. And though it was an entirely different kind of enthusiasm, Sparky was starting to take on some of Ceff's mannerisms. The way he held his head and shoulders, and, well, his aluminum foil trident, only reinforced the likeness. It was uncanny.

The toddler-sized leather jacket, so like my own, was also super cute. It was pretty obvious who his heroes were. My heart swelled and, for just a moment, I forgot how to breathe.

"It's okay," Jinx whispered in my ear. I hadn't even noticed how close she'd managed to get to me. Weird. Either Forneus was teaching her some tricks or my friend was becoming a ninja. Or, just maybe, I had been distracted by the one thing, okay maybe two things, I loved as much as her. "He's totally safe. No zombies. No bad guys. He's happy and healthy. Not even a scratch."

Thank Mab for best friends and their bizarre ability to read your mind without any psychic abilities whatsoever.

"Thanks to you," I said. "Thanks for watching him."

"And thanks to my sexy almost-husband," Jinx said, devouring Forneus with a look.

"Ew, um, do I have to thank him?" I said.

I'd rather suck rotten eggs. I was trying to be friends with Forneus, but being his almost-almost-sister-in-law wasn't something that came naturally. In fact, I'm pretty sure it would have been more normal for us to tear each other to shreds.

"I had to work," she said, cocking a hip and waving with the spatula that was still in her well-manicured hand. "You know, in the office, the thing that keeps this roof over our heads? Forneus was the one who kept Sparky entertained."

"Okay, fine, I'll thank him," I said, rolling my eyes.

It was hard to hold a grudge against a guy who probably spent most of his day playing with glitter ponies and pretending to be an elephant, or a tiger, or a cephalopod for my kid. Hmm, maybe we had been watching too many nature documentaries lately.

"Good," she said, with a wink. "While you're at it, try to get over whatever nonsense you two are always fighting about. You know, before the wedding."

Right, double wedding. How could I forget? Thankfully, I was relieved of apology duty when Ceff strode out of the bathroom in all his kingly glory. Saved by the kelpie.

He wore only a towel that hung low on his hips, showing off the wide expanse of his chest, a trim waist, and a well-muscled abdomen. I reluctantly pulled my eyes from the narrow v disappearing into the towel and met his heated gaze.

"Did someone mention a wedding?" Forneus asked, following Sparky in from the living room.

Oh, goody. Now the whole gang was here.

"Actually, now that we're all together, I think we should discuss our zombie problem," I said.

"I will get dressed," Ceff said.

I frowned. Okay, I might even have pouted, but those were words I strongly disliked hearing from my fiancé.

It didn't take Ceff long to don a pair of jeans. He was still pulling a shirt over damp hair as he strolled out of our bedroom.

"Since a kelpie has Ivy's tongue, maybe you can catch us up to speed?" Jinx asked, blinking at Ceff.

Ceff grinned, but nodded. Once we got Sparky settled with earbuds and an audiobook, we filled our friends in on the zombie infestation over at the glaistig's old stomping grounds. My hands clenched into fists while discussing what we found in the dumpster, but it wasn't just the theft of those remains that upset me.

I was still haunted by a dryad's ruby red slipper. Visions had a tendency to linger and that one wasn't going away any time soon.

"From all accounts, it would appear this necromancer is the true threat, and is the one violating Sir Gaius' exclusive contracts to harvest Harborsmouth's corpses," Forneus said.

"This necromancer dude sounds creepy," Jinx said, biting her lip. "Who bleeds people to raise zombies and then chops up their body parts and stuffs them in a dumpster?"

"It is rather diabolical," Forneus said, a touch of admiration in his voice.

"It is also blatantly breaking the First Law," Ceff said. "Raising zombies, especially zombie faeries, to walk where humans might see them threatens all supernatural kind. What if it brings the faerie court's assassins here?"

I shivered. The last thing I needed was the Moordenaar crawling all over my city. I rubbed my side, the phantom pain a memory of my last run-in with the faerie assassins. I'd been shot through the heart, liver, and stomach with their arrows. I'd died. If it hadn't been for a couple of magic apples that I'd smuggled from Emain Ablach, I'd be one of the corpses currently at this zombie master's mercy.

Now that was a chilling thought.

"I don't think it wise to gain the council's attention," Ceff said. "Not with Ivy's connection to the Unseelie court."

I shivered again, this time breaking into cold sweats. Being reminded that your mother is an uber powerful homicidal maniac will do that.

The phone rang and I jumped. I reached for my phone hoping for good news. I could use a positive distraction right about now.

"We have a problem," Torn said.

So much for good news.

CHAPTER 17

I arrived at the carnival's service entrance to find an agitated cat sidhe lord. That made two of us.

"All of the body parts have gone missing," Torn said, hissing. "The dead faerie's belongings too."

Crap. Just my luck. I wouldn't be getting any more visions from these victims. The dumpster had been scrubbed.

"How did this happen?" Ceff asked, his voice holding a threat just below the surface. Okay, maybe three of us were angry. We'd left Jinx, Forneus, and Sparky to finish their dinner, and hold down the fort, but there was no way Ceff was leaving my side. "They deserved a proper burial. Now they are lost."

Oh, yeah. He was definitely angry.

"And we might have gained new clues, or at least learned a bit more about the victims," I said, arms folded across my chest. "If we hit too many dead ends, I might even have tried for another vision."

It wouldn't have been the first case where I'd pulled an all-nighter, touching object after object in search of the truth. Visions weren't my first choice, especially not when dealing with victims of violent death, but it was an option that I no longer had. Someone else had taken that choice away from me, leaving me surprisingly pissed off. I may not enjoy using my psychometry, but I enjoyed others making decisions for me even less.

Ceff and I weren't the only ones who were angry. Torn's nostrils were flaring, his breathing loud and ragged as he bounced on the balls of his feet, ready to pounce on anyone who dared come too close. He hissed, his ears pressed flat back against his head.

"Come on," I said, holding up gloved hands. "Let's all calm down. Losing those bodies, those people, is a setback, but it's all the more reason to find out what the necromancer has planned and stop him."

"And kill him," Torn said.

It wasn't a question. I nodded.

"Probably," I said. "Now tell us what happened."

According to Torn, he'd watched the front gate, because it was where the action was at. Most of the zombies that were entering from outside the carnival grounds were shambling in through the front gate. Thankfully, those were mostly small faeries, so far. The larger zombies we'd seen had come from the carnival fae's own graveyard, but that was now empty. It made sense to watch the front gate, but that didn't make it less frustrating to have missed someone stealing the bodies from the service entrance parking lot.

"And you're sure it wasn't your cleanup crew?" I asked.

"No," he said. "As soon as one of my cats arrived to watch the front gates, I returned to the service entrance to wait for our crew. When I got here, the dumpster was empty. I called my people and they were still dealing with a job on the other side of town."

That wasn't ominous or anything.

"What kind of job?" I asked.

"None of your business, princess," he said.

I fisted my hands and I stalked forward. Torn wasn't cowed, but he did roll his eyes and elaborate. I relaxed my hands, but kept a wide stance, ready for a fight. I was sick to death of secrets.

"Let's just say that some of Club Nexus' clientele get sloppy after a night of drinking," he said. "My cats have been known to follow them. Sometimes we even clean up their messes for a price."

"And a little blackmail, I'm sure," I said, narrowing my eyes.

Torn shrugged.

"The point is, my men were busy and didn't make it here in time to gather any clues or scrub the scene for human eyes," he said.

The skin at my neck itched. Speaking of eyes, I still couldn't shake the feeling that we were being watched.

Before I could ask Torn if he'd placed any cats here as lookouts, a woman leapt from the roof of the maintenance building to the broken pavement. Ceff reached for his trident, but I held up a gloved hand.

"Wait," I said. "I know her."

Her clothes were threadbare and covered a bit more skin than the last time I'd seen her, but I wasn't mistaken. I'd recognize this particular succubus no matter what she was wearing.

"Delilah," I said with a wary nod.

"Misss Granger," she said.

"You got any idea what's going on here?" I asked.

The question was vague, but I'd learned that when questioning witnesses, it was best to cast a wide net. I also wasn't sure that Delilah was just a witness. I flicked my wrist, palming one of my knives. If she did turn on us, I'd need a weapon I could use from a few yards away. Getting up close and person with Delilah was not an option. Thankfully, she kept her distance.

"I can ssshow you," she said, cocking a hip and gesturing toward the side of the building.

I was beginning to hate that alley and the nightmares that it led to.

"If you want to show us the graveyard, don't bother," I said. "We've seen it."

She smirked and laughed, the movement drawing Torn's attention to her chest.

"I know," she said. "I sssaw you. But you didn't find him. You didn't sssee him."

"Him, as in, the necromancer?" I asked.

Now we were getting somewhere.

"He isss more than that," she said with a nod. "And he mussst be killed."

"I like her," Torn said.

Of course, he did. Delilah was a female Torn, wearing a bit less leather. If I left it up to them, we'd be neck deep in zombies and necromancer blood right now. Either that or an orgy.

I blinked and returned my attention to the case. For once, happy to focus on our zombie problem.

"If we wanted to kill this necromancer, and that's a big if," I said, ignoring Torn's muttered "no fun" comment. "We'd need to know where to find him. I'm guessing he's inside the Haunted House ride where all of the zombies are headed."

Delilah nodded.

"And inside his portal," I said.

Her eyes widened.

"Yeah, I know about the portal," I said. "At least, I know that he uses a portal. I saw that much in a vision, but I don't know anything about what's on the other side."

The succubus took an involuntary step back.

"But I think she does," Torn said.

He tilted his head and watched Delilah closely.

"It'sss a long ssstory," she said.

"I'm all ears," I said.

CHAPTER 18

Delilah had been spying on the necromancer and his zombie creations for a long time. In fact, she'd been watching since the beginning.

The Green Lady had banished the succubus and I'd freed her, but Delilah didn't go far. In all the ways that mattered, she never really left. While she valued her freedom, she missed her surrogate family. She might no longer be one of the Green Lady's loyal subjects, but she would always remain loyal to the carnival fae. She would not run from the glaistig's territory. This had been her home.

And when the Green Lady up and left in the night, Delilah might have gone with them. But she knew the glaistig's terrible secret, the way that the faerie queen had solved the problem of where to bury the carnival fae when she'd run out of space. The Green Lady had made a bargain with a necromancer.

To make the situation worse, the man wasn't just any old necromancer. Our necromancer was a lich. Scratch that. He was a lich king.

In Harborsmouth, when it rains monsters, it pours.

I'd need more info from Father Michael's occult library, but from what we could piece together, a lich is a scary powerful sorcerer obsessed with becoming immortal. They used blood rites to transform their bodies into a skeletal, corpse-like creature that looked similar to the most ancient vampires.

Unlike vampires, they did not die to become a monster. They were not truly undead. Their magic, in fact, prevented death, allowing them, with enough bloody sacrifices, to extend their lives indefinitely.

I had no idea how to fight such a thing.

"Do you believe her?" Ceff asked, keeping his voice low while Torn and Delilah flirted with each other.

"I do," I said.

Delilah was a conundrum. She'd saved my life more than once, but she also betrayed me in the worst way possible.

That had been at the order of her master, the Green Lady, but it still rankled and made her hard for me to trust. So, I did what I'd done with other unreliable witnesses. I asked myself what her motives were. It was clear that she appreciated me freeing her. She was also loyal to her old friends within the carnival fae. Pretty sure the latter was the most important.

"Then we need to find a way to kill a lich," he said. "I suggest we pay Father Michael a visit."

"Good," I said, nodding. "I wanted to check in with him anyway. We've got a lot of dead faeries walking around and now we have missing victims, parts of them anyway, that might still turn up. When this is all over, I want to know that someone will give these faeries a proper burial."

That was a favor best asked in person. Some things just shouldn't be done over the phone. I wasn't looking forward to that conversation, but I couldn't put it off until later. With a lich king, a magic portal, and a zombie horde, there might not be a later.

CHAPTER 19

Unfortunately, our trip to visit Father Michael was delayed.

"You need to hear this, princess," Torn. He turned to Delilah and ran a hand up and down her arm. "Go on, sweetheart."

"The portal hasss a guardian," she said.

"Great," I said. Of course, there were more monsters to deal with. As if a lich king and his growing zombie horde wasn't bad enough. I was almost missing that time, less than a day ago, when all I had to worry about were zombie gerbils and a pissed off vampire. "Any idea how to defeat this guardian? It's weaknesses?"

"Pretty sure it doesn't have any weaknesses," Torn said, eyes twinkling with excitement.

"And why's that?" I asked, fidgeting with the knives strapped to my forearms.

Torn wasn't the only one with something up his sleeve. But I was pretty sure whatever secret he was about to reveal was likely to get me dead. He was enjoying this way too much.

"Because, princess," he said, pausing dramatically. "The portal guardian is a dragon."

Well, if that wasn't a punch in the gut. On the upside, it can't get any weirder than a dragon guardian.

I was sure that had to be the worst possible news of the day. I was wrong.

"Zzzombie dragon," Delilah said.

Of course, it was an Oberon damn zombie dragon.

"This I've got to see," I muttered.

"Much as I'd like to fight a dragon, princess," Torn said. "I was hoping not to get eaten today."

Delilah sidled up and nibbled on one of his scarred ears.

"That'sss too bad," she said, licking her lips.

"I stand corrected," he said.

Ew, gross.

"So, um, how big is this dragon?" I asked.

My chest felt strangely tight, like I was being slowly squeezed to death. It wasn't a pleasant sensation.

"Zombie dragon," Ceff said.

I wasn't sure if he was correcting me or just trying to process the fact that the lich king's portal was guarded by a zombie dragon. That was going to take some getting used to. I'd seen a whole lot of crazy things over the years—thanks a lot, second sight—but I'd never even considered that dragons might be real. My brain couldn't even come up with a reasonable picture for what this guardian might look like.

"Is it bigger than a breadbox?" Torn asked, scorching Delilah with his gaze.

The succubus started to reach below his waist, and I threw one of my knives. It didn't hit anyone, but it did get their attention.

Delilah shrugged.

"Bessst to ssshow you," she said.

And with that, she sauntered down what was becoming my least favorite alley in Harborsmouth, second only to the one beside Club Nexus where Torn held court.

"This is going to be so much fun," Torn said, rubbing his hands together.

I wasn't sure if he meant following behind the succubus' curvaceous derriere, which she was swaying with mesmerizing skill, or if he was talking about facing a zombie dragon. Probably, best not to think about it.

I loped ahead, trying to catch up with Delilah. I still had questions.

"So, this zombie dragon is at the portal?" I asked. "Guarding the way into this Necropolis?"

"I will ssshow you," she said.

"Yeah, um, there's just one thing," I said. "There's still the little problem of this lich dude's zombie horde. If the dragon is guarding the portal, and this portal is located inside the Haunted House ride, how are we supposed to get a close look at it without, you know, the zombies eating our brains?"

"I don't think they really eat brains, princess," Torn said.

I shot him a glare and, for once, he shut up.

"This wasss my home," Delilah said, lifting her chin. "I know a way."

CHAPTER 20

Delilah hadn't been lying about knowing a way into the Haunted House. Too bad she failed to mention it required crawling into a maintenance hatch.

I closed my eyes and took a deep breath, psyching myself up.

"We just crept past more than twenty zombies, princess," Torn said. "How can you be nervous about a tiny door?"

I opened my eyes and forced myself to look at the metal opening. Tiny was an understatement. I wasn't even sure how Ceff was going to squeeze through. Torn on the other hand, wouldn't have any trouble.

"Easy for you to say," I said. "You can shapeshift into a cat."

Torn shrugged. He got down on his hands and knees, winked at Delilah, who seemed intrigued by the position, and shifted.

"Meow."

Jerk. I wasn't claustrophobic, not really. My problem was with the potential for unwanted visions that came with squeezing into tight spaces. I checked that my shirt was tucked into my jeans and my leather jacket was zipped all the way.

The zombies were all staggering in through the ride's entrance, following the metal track into the building. But that didn't mean that the maintenance hatch hadn't ever been witness to something disturbing. Knowing the glaistig, it was nearly a given.

"Give us a moment," Ceff said, frowning at Torn.

The cat lowered his eyelids in a baleful glare and, with the twitch of his scarred tail, leapt inside the hatch. Delilah followed, giving us a rather disturbing view as she writhed and wiggled her way into the ride's ductwork.

I turned to Ceff and gasped. He closed the distance between us, pressing his lips to my chin. When I didn't flinch with a vision, I could feel his brow raise, but he slid his mouth along my jaw, ending in a long, lingering kiss. He pulled back reluctantly, but not fully.

Ceff rested his forehead against mine.

"Ready?" he asked.

"Yes," I said. "Let's go see what a zombie dragon looks like."

My courage lasted all of five minutes. Never wear boots and a leather jacket to shimmy down an airshaft. I had to close my eyes and calm my breathing multiple times before coming to an intersection where the maintenance shaft widened.

There was a grid set into the center of the intersection which Torn, Delilah, and Ceff now hovered over.

"What have we got?" I asked, trying to keep my voice from shaking.

It wasn't easy. My nerves were jangling my heart right out of my chest. Not only had my jacket caught on bolts and screw heads on the way here, threatening me with visions, but the death magic in the air was making my skin itch, and the incessant music coming from below was damn creepy. Apparently, even though the ride cars weren't moving along the tracks, the power was still on, allowing the Haunted House's discordant theme music to play on an endless, nightmarish loop.

I was living in a freaking horror movie.

"Another hatch," Ceff said, pointing at the grid.

Torn didn't answer since he was still in his cat form, using the opportunity to curl up in Delilah's lap which also happened to place him up close and personal with her prodigious bosom. The man was incorrigible and purring up a storm.

"Wait," I said, inching forward for a better look.

"Thisss way," Delilah said, removing her hand from petting Torn long enough to point at the hatch we were all gathered around.

I really hoped the shaft was reinforced here or we were all going to lose whatever surprise advantage we had and go toppling to our deaths. And if we died here, I had no doubt what would happen to our bodies. I wanted to see this portal, not go walking blindly through it.

"That's the ride track," I said with a frown. "I thought the zombies were following the track."

"No," Delilah said, shaking her head, and other parts, making Torn purr even louder. "Jusst at the entranccce."

"Oh, okay," I said.

I still wasn't eager to go down there. The ride cars weren't moving along the track, and there were no zombies in sight, but the creepy Haunted House music was playing, and the place was dark, even to my faerie-improved vision. Who knows what we'd run into down there?

Torn jumped off Delilah's lap and pawed at the grate. Yeah, yeah, no time for dilly-dallying or panic attacks. Not with a super cool zombie dragon to go check out.

Delilah untwisted the screws from each corner, keeping her eyes on Torn the entire time and somehow making reverse carpentry seem sexy. Say what you want, but that girl had skills. When she was done, Ceff lifted the panel and set it aside. He made it look effortless, but I'm pretty sure that thing weighed more than me.

As soon as the opening was clear, Torn leapt, shifting from cat to man so that he landed on two feet. Show off.

I suppose, under different conditions, I might have ripped off my jacket, unfurled my wings, after they tore out through my back which was not as smooth and easy as Torn's shapeshifting, not by a long shot, and flown to the ground below. But my nerves were shot and the ductwork was too cramped for me to unfurl my wings. I'd just have to jump down like the human I'd been raised to be, albeit with a bit more grace.

The drop to the bottom was pretty elegant. Falling on my butt when an animatronic witch jumped out at me was not. Great. Not only was there creepy music, but the Haunted House's motion-triggered effects were still fully functional.

"You owe me ten bucks," Torn said, holding a hand, palm out, toward Delilah.

"Seriously, you guys?" I asked, standing and brushing fake spiderwebs off my jeans.

"That'sss not how I plan to pay," Delilah said, leaning into Torn and running talon-like fingernails up and down his chest.

I turned to Ceff whose lip was twitching as he fought to hide a grin.

"Really?" I asked, throwing my hands up in the air.

"I did not see the sensor," he said, losing his battle with the grin. "Apparently, they did."

"And bet on me!" I pseudo whispered.

Even with the creepy music playing, I didn't dare shout. Not with some of these tunnels crawling with zombies.

"Did you see her face?" Torn asked. "Priceless."

I glowered and rolled my eyes. It was an Olympian feat, but I'd had a lot of practice. Hanging out with Torn had made me an expert eye roller. I suppose if I died here, they could put that on my tombstone. Ivy Granger, psychic detective, hero of Harborsmouth, and eye rolling gold medalist. Of course, if I died here, I'd become a zombie and never get a headstone. Small favors and all that.

"If everyone is done making fun of me, how about we go get a good look at a dragon," I said.

"Zzzombie dragon," Delilah said.

"Whatever," I said, lifting one shoulder.

"Thisss way," she said.

"Hey, how far are we from the zombies?" I asked, glancing around the dark tunnel.

I tried to ignore the animatronic witch, but that was hard to do while yanking one of my throwing knives from its forehead. I'd scored a direct hit, not that doing so would save me from Torn's teasing. I was never going to hear the end of this.

"Not far," Delilah said, a frown marring her porcelain complexion. "Look."

She strode over to the tunnel wall, peeled back a thick layer of latex blood, and pointed at a small hole. I leaned forward, careful not to touch Delilah or the wall, and stared into the adjacent hallway. The narrow space was lined in mirrors and filled with zombies. The visual effect, an infinity of zombies of all shapes and sizes, sucked the air from my lungs.

Since I'd so recently shamed myself by falling on my butt, I was careful not to lurch back from the opening, but it was a near thing. By the time I moved away from the wall, my heart was doing a tap dance to match the creepy Haunted House music which was like a kid turning the crank on a Jack-in-the-Box while on crack.

"Can they see us?" I asked when I regained my voice.

"No," she said, shaking her head.

"Good," I said.

The tunnels in both directions were a black void, dark even to faerie eyes. We didn't have a flashlight, but we had the next best thing. I let some of my fear leach to the surface of my skin, emanating enough of a glow that we were unlikely to break our necks on our way to the portal.

Ceff nodded his approval and Delilah started down the tunnel. Torn grinned from ear to ear and quickened his step, nearly clicking his heels with joy. I shook my head. We were going to go see a dragon. What was there to be so happy about?

Thankfully, the portal wasn't far. Before rounding another corner, Delilah gestured for me to turn off the wisp glow. It didn't take long to see why.

In the center of the building, in a large, cavernous room made to look like a cave filled with gigantic spiders and their webs, stood the portal. The gateway was large enough for even the zombie centaurs to pass through without ducking their decaying heads, and it swirled sickeningly with a blue, spectral light.

I scratched at my arms absently and surveyed the artificial cave beyond. Faux spiderwebs crisscrossed the space, holding the weight of giant plastic spiders and their cocooned victims. The cocoons were soaked with fake blood and I had to keep reminding myself that it wasn't real.

The thing was, some of this was real. The zombies weren't part of the show, stumbling and crawling their way to the portal. Their stench was an unavoidable reminder that they weren't just people, and pets, wearing makeup and costumes.

As horrific as the scene was, this wasn't all that we'd come to see.

"Dragon?" I mouthed, not quite willing to risk a whisper, even with the incessant music echoing through the tunnel.

But Delilah only pointed at the portal. I focused on the swirl of blue until I caught sight of motion beyond the portal's threshold. A dark form emerged, rolled, rising up from the depths. It was like watching sharks swimming just beneath the ocean's surface.

Guarding the entrance to the Necropolis, watching hungrily as every zombie passed through the portal, paced a mountain of scales and claws. Even through the portal, I could see that those claws were made for rending flesh from bone.

I swallowed hard, mouth going dry, as the dragon, a real undead zombie dragon, prowled back and forth. The dragon's muscles rolled beneath black scales that shimmered where they caught and reflected the gateway's spectral glow.

A zombie stumbled over the bones that littered the Necropolis and the dragon lunged, snarling and snapping its jaws. It struck fast as a viper and its jaw muscles were impressive, but the rows of razor-like teeth were the most disturbing. Or so I thought.

The dragon's long, lizard tongue lashed out, flickering between sharp teeth that were the most terrifying thing I could imagine. Then it unfurled its wings. They were leathery, bat-like, tattered from decay, and dark as midnight, except where they were shot through with the contrasting brightness of moonlit bone. This was by far the most monstrous, most powerful creature I'd ever seen.

Oh, yeah. That was going to be a problem.

I crept away from the gate and back down the tunnel. I might be a faerie, the daughter of a wisp king and queen Mab herself, but at that moment I stumbled along like a mundane human. Oberon knows, I tried, but fear still took hold. I'm convinced that there is something deep in our brainstems, whispering in our very DNA, the knowledge that whether human or faerie, we would never stand a chance against a fully-grown dragon.

So, I did what any sensible creature would do. I ran.

When I could breathe again, I met the eyes of my friends and my beloved, under the hatch that might, if our luck held, lead us to safety.

I was aware of the irony that the claustrophobic ductwork that had seemed so threatening moments ago now held only the hope of escape. Funny how a zombie dragon changes things.

I had no idea how we could defeat a creature that huge, that powerful, or how we could get past the zombie dragon, enter the Necropolis, and destroy the lich king and his zombie horde. Right at this moment, I was unsure of so many things. But one thing was certain.

"We need a priest."

CHAPTER 21

Torn and Delilah decided to stay behind and continue to spy on the zombies milling through the carnival grounds. I was a bit dubious about that team-up, but I wasn't even sure about the logistics of a succubus entering a church, and I couldn't expect my priest friend to carry his occult library all the way to Private Eye. Things were so much easier when I could pop around the corner and stop by The Emporium for research on rare creatures, but those days were over.

Ceff and I left the cat sidhe and succubus behind and made our way up Joysen Hill. It was strangely quiet for this part of town, as if even the seasoned criminals of the supernatural community were laying low, sensing trouble on the wind.

Rather than easing the tension in my shoulders, the lack of obvious threats made me even jumpier than usual. Considering that Joysen Hill was the nexus for the city's most violent crimes, the vile underbelly of the supernatural underworld where the most dangerous and immoral of the fae and the undead came fang to toe with Harborsmouth's most disenfranchised, we should have been accosted or been witness to some evil deed at least once by now.

"This is creepy," I said, scanning the area for threats.

The leather of my gloves creaked as my grip tightened on my knives. Even though my glamour, a new lifesaving skill I'd picked up in the crucible of the wisp court, could conceal my weapons, I probably needn't have bothered.

I'd only ever seen one cop on The Hill. Most of the city's finest chose to cast a blind eye to the criminal wrongdoings here. Not that I could blame them. More than one don't-look-here spell was active here in the East End. Even if the cops patrolled these streets, they'd never see the monsters that lurked in the shadows or the ones who hid in plain sight.

That's why I'd started my own patrols, even working at times with Master Janus' people. The Hunters' Guild was a secret society descended from the Knights Templar. They were a rare group of, mostly, humans who knew about the existence of supernaturals, and their job was to protect humans from vampires and faeries who crossed the line, usually succumbing to bloodlust or deciding that humans were super fun playthings to torture.

I'd first been introduced to the Hunters' Guild by Jenna Lehane, a young woman and kick-ass Hunter who had sworn to protect the innocent from supernatural threats. Unfortunately, Jenna was also sworn to a brotherhood that frowned on turning on each other. So, when Jenna found out a Hunter had assaulted Jinx, she'd done the right thing, and ended up shipped off to Europe. The Guild had come in handy, especially during our battle with the Wild Hunt, but I missed Jenna.

"Perhaps, your nighttime excursions have had the desired effect," Ceff said.

I shook my head. I'd like to believe that, but I knew that for every crime we solved, for every person we saved, more evil would sprout from the soil of The Hill. It was like the vampires who owned most of the Joysen Hill real estate had seeded the East End with some kind of tainted magic beans. Who knows? Maybe, they had. Stranger things have happened.

Speaking of strange, there was a church grim prancing atop the Gothic spires of the church, playing chase with one of the gargoyles who guarded the stone parapets. Church grims are small, adorable faeries that look similar to baby lambs with curly hair the color of milk. That wasn't the strange part. What was unusual was that the grim had stuck around.

Church grims are death portents, appearing only when a child is about to die. When this grim first appeared, fluttering around the church's ceiling, we'd known that at least one of Father Michael's flock was in grave danger. Things had turned out alright in the end, but it had been a close call. It had taken a lot of work to reassure the faerie families that their children were safe. We'd been so busy, none of us noticed that the grim never left.

So, now Sacred Heart Church had its own resident church grim and the only thing the playful faerie liked more than snuggling with Galliel, the gorgeous unicorn who lived here in seclusion, was chasing the pigeons and gargoyles who roosted on the spires that reached toward the heavens.

I suppose a unicorn should also seem strange, but Galliel and I had bonded the moment we met. It was love at first sight, and we'd been each other's family ever since. If it wasn't for the fact that the little guy was in hiding—unicorn horn is a magically potent delicacy that meant Galliel's life would always be in danger from poachers—I would have offered to take him home. Of course, I'd have to get a bigger apartment. Maybe, Ceff had a point when he said we should go house hunting.

Father Michael and Galliel welcomed us as soon as we entered the church, the latter knocking me on my butt in his enthusiasm for ear scratches. It was the second time today that I'd landed on my backside, but I didn't mind. I loved the unicorn and our cuddles. Galliel was my oasis of light in the turbulent darkness that was my everyday life.

He didn't even give me nightmarish visions, which was a major bonus. Galliel did, however, like to trap me on the floor while I showered him with affection. Normally, I'd be game, but we had a lich king, a zombie dragon, and an angry vampire to deal with.

Thankfully, with far too many giggles on my part, we managed to get Galliel off me long enough to relocate to Father Michael's office. The priest kept an extensive occult library in his office. The collection was impressive, and more than one of those books were pilfered from the Vatican. I wasn't the only one of my friends with a colorful past.

Now that we were in the privacy of Father Michael's office, Ceff and I were filling in the priest on what we knew.

Father Michael deserved to know that his congregation may be facing a new deadly threat, and we needed information. People think that all a hero needs is a strong sword, but, in my experience, she needs good friends and good intel.

"Sir Gaius came to your office?" Father Michael asked, head bobbing over a notebook in an excited bird-like motion. "That is most interesting."

"Oh, it gets much more interesting, padre," I said.

"Do I dare ask how this meeting with the vampire master ended?" he asked, looking up from his desk.

"What?" I asked. "We still had all of our blood on the inside. I'd call that a win. Gaius was pissed about his harvesting rights. It could have gone worse."

Much worse.

"Ivy made a promise to find out who was responsible for the graverobbing," Ceff said. "Hence our need for haste."

"Ah, you should really stop doing that, my dear," Father Michael said.

I rolled my eyes. Well, I tried to. I stopped midway due to the stabbing pain in my skull. It was like little goblins were using tiny pickaxes on my optic nerve. Stupid bargains and their side-effects.

I must have let out a low moan, because Galliel nudged me and licked my face. It tickled my nose and I sneezed, surprising both of us.

"As you can see, she already has a headache," Ceff said. "It will get worse, fatigue and pain tearing her apart, until we find the person responsible and notify Sir Gaius."

I shrugged one shoulder, not meeting Ceff's concerned gaze.

"It's a case," I said. "I'll solve it. It's what I do."

"We know precisely what you do, dear," Father Michael said. "That is why we are concerned."

I let out a snort but refrained from shaking my head. As much as I hated to admit it, they were right. I was too quick to do what I believed to be the right thing, usually putting myself directly into danger. And if Sir Gaius walked into my office tomorrow and threatened Jinx, I'd do it all over again.

Jinx wasn't just my best friend. She was my sister. She was my heart. Jinx represented all of things that were good about humans, the things I'd come to believe anyway, and I couldn't lose her. If there was a choice between watching Jinx be harmed or taking on a bad bargain, I'd accept that debt every time.

In fact, an entire new family had crept into my life, giving me more and more friends to protect. I used to think I'd die alone. I'd been a fool. If I were to die, it would be saving lives. My family had grown, but so had the risks.

"The case isn't the part you should be concerned about," I said.

"Yes, of course, there is the matter of the zombies," Father Michael said, leaning forward and licking his lips.

The priest was obsessed with demonology, but he was also a sucker for any kind of supernatural knowledge. I'm sure he'd get a kick out of hearing about the great zombie gerbil hunt, but we didn't have time. Ceff was right about that. We were on a deadline.

So, I filled him in on the bodies in the dumpster, the empty graves, my vision, and the zombies staggering their way through the abandoned carnival, heading toward a magic portal that led to the Necropolis. It was a lot to take in.

I was careful not to mention Delilah, since we couldn't afford to get sidetracked. If I mentioned the succubus, Father Michael was likely to ramble on about the demonic origins of that particular kind of fae. We couldn't afford the distraction.

"We must enter the lich king's realm," Ceff said. "He no longer needs to perform his blood rites here in Harborsmouth."

I nodded, lips pressed in a hard line.

"With his plans set in motion, all the lich king has to do is sit back in his pocket dimension and reap the rewards," I said.

"The residual magic in the faerie corpses," Father Michael said. "Fascinating."

"Yes, as zombies, the dead will literally walk the magic to his doorstep," I said. "Making the lich even more powerful."

"Oh, dear," he muttered. "Even if you weren't in the thrall of a bargain, you would need to make haste. But I believe you still have time."

"Time, padre?" I asked.

"Time to defeat the lich," he said absently, shuffling through books and scrolls. "Before he absorbs too much magic."

He got up, pacing and squinting at the shelves that lined his office. His head bobbed as he searched for what he was looking for.

"Before he gets too powerful," I said, the direness of our situation sinking in.

That certainly upped the timetable.

"According to this, there are ways to defeat a lich," he said. "It will not be easy, but I have faith in you."

Father Michael lifted a scroll that bore the Vatican's seal. Usually, I'd tease when the priest hauled out one of the obviously stolen manuscripts, but I was a bit busy worrying about liches and zombie dragons while petting a unicorn. My life really is weird.

"It gets worse," I said.

"How can it possibly be worse than zombies, blood sacrifices, and a lich king?" Father Michael asked, twitching nervously.

"There is the matter of the dragon," Ceff said.

Father Michael gaped. I snorted and continued to pet Galliel.

"Told you it was worse," I said. "And that's not all."

"Wait," Father Michael said, easing himself into the chair behind his desk. He'd been running his hands through his hair which now stuck out in every direction. "I think I might need to sit for this."

"Ready?" I asked.

"Okay, yes, ready as I'll ever be," he said. "Not that I can possibly see how this could get any worse."

"The dragon guarding the lich king's portal isn't just an ordinary dragon," I said. Okay, even I couldn't believe I'd said that with a straight face. "The guardian is a zombie. A zombie dragon."

"I stand corrected," he said. "I guess I should have known."

"Why's that?" I asked.

"Things are always worse where you're concerned," he said.

Galliel whinnied, and Ceff hid a grin. Traitors.

"Any idea how to kill a zombie dragon?" I asked.

"You don't," he said.

"Not helpful," I said.

"What I mean is, you cannot kill the dragon directly," he said. "It is clear in all of the lore that killing a dragon requires an epic quest."

"Which we do not have time for," Ceff said, frowning.

"Right," Father Michael said. "But you do not have to kill this dragon. It is already dead."

"Because it's a zombie?" I asked. "Doesn't that make my job harder?"

"No, look here," he said, pushing an open book toward me and pointing at the page. "If you kill a lich, all of his creations, every zombie that he has animated, will cease to be a zombie."

"So, they'll die, again," I said.

"Yes," he said. "Their corpses will no longer be animated."

"That's a great plan except for one tiny detail," I said. "The zombie dragon guards the portal."

"Then you will need to find another way into the Necropolis," he said.

"I'm guessing that will be a tad difficult," I said.

"As will killing a lich king," he said.

"Awesome," I said.

CHAPTER 22

As we left Sacred Heart, my phone chimed. I pulled it from my jacket pocket and Ceff raised an eyebrow.

"Text from Forneus," I said. I stared at the screen, eyes going wide. "He says he knows another way into the Necropolis."

I'd sent out a group text asking if my friends had any ideas on how to sneak into the Necropolis. Not that I had high hopes.

Father Michael had been able to provide useful information on how to kill the lich king, which would solve our zombie problem and make me square with Gaius, but we hadn't found anything helpful on how to get inside the Necropolis. The only gateway we knew of was guarded by a zombie dragon that I hoped never to lay eyes on again.

"That sounds promising," Ceff said.

I called Forneus and put him on speaker.

"A back door, for real?" I asked.

We didn't have time for niceties.

"For reals," Jinx said.

Apparently, we weren't the only ones using speakerphone. I could even hear Sparky playing in the background, the little munchkin. My chest swelled, happy my kid was safe.

Forneus cleared his throat, bringing my attention back to our dragon problem. If I wanted to keep my kid, all of the city's kids, safe, I should listen to him.

"There is a doorway to the Necropolis in Highgate Cemetery," Forneus said.

"There's a gateway to the Necropolis in a place called Highgate?" I asked.

"Right?" Jinx asked. "Really makes you think about the term lich gate too."

She had a point. But Forneus continued on as if our comments were merely trivial. I suppose, in the grand scheme of things, they were.

"At least, it was there when I negotiated a territorial dispute in the cemetery back in the late 19th century," he said. "Have I ever mentioned how tedious the fetch and the banshee clans can be?"

That was probably an interesting story, but my brain finally placed the cemetery's location.

"Wait, Highgate Cemetery, as in London?" I asked.

"Of course," Forneus said, letting out an exasperated sigh.

"How are we supposed to get to London?" I asked.

There's no way I was flying across the ocean in a tin can. Too much iron. Not to mention all the opportunities for being overwhelmed by psychic visions. And how were we supposed to smuggle all of our weapons through the TSA screening? Nope, we'd have to find an alternate way to London.

"What about Torn?" Jinx asked.

There was a shuffling on the other end of the line as if someone was covering the phone and having a muffled conversation. Forneus wasn't fond of Torn, not with the cat sidhe lord's relentless flirting with Jinx. But I had to admit, my best friend had a point.

If there was a way to travel through the shadows from Harborsmouth to London, Torn would know about it. It was like he could sweet talk the shadows into anything. If there was a secret pathway, Torn would be able to access it.

"Torn and Delilah are keeping watch over the glaistig's former territory," Ceff said.

"Delilah?" Jinx asked, voice raising an octave, rapidly approaching a screech. "As in the succubus who ruffied me? The bitch who almost got me killed?"

I winced, rubbing the back of my neck with gloved hands. Mab's bones. This could get ugly. Jinx had every right to be angry at Delilah. But there was too much at stake.

Plus, deep down, I couldn't blame the succubus. I wanted to, if only to shed some of my own guilt, but Delilah had been following orders. Knowing the feudal system most faeries lived under, and the magic that enforced the power of our leaders, she may not have had any choice.

"Um, yeah," I said.

"You did not die, my love," Forneus murmured. "You are safe."

My ears burned with embarrassment. I felt like a voyeur on that private conversation. Sadly, I needed to intrude further.

"We've all done things we regret," I said, my voice small and pleading. "Delilah was acting on the Green Lady's orders when she did those things. I think...I want to give her a second chance."

We all deserve a second chance. If I stopped believing that, I'd question all the good things in my life. That way lies madness.

"Fine," Jinx said. "But if she double-crosses us, I want first dibs on shooting her."

"Deal," I said, slumping in relief.

My best friend was one of the most patient, kind, forgiving people on the planet, but I did not envy any fool who dared cross her twice. Jinx may be human, but she was a damn good shot with a crossbow. Who says you need magical powers to kick butt?

The relief was short-lived, the weight of the bargain sucking the air from my lungs. I needed to stop doing that. It was way too easy to forget that bargains and promises were no longer nothing to worry about. I wasn't human, not even half-human, as I'd believed. Being a faerie, and being bound to our laws, was still taking some getting used to.

"I'll talk to Torn and get back to you," I said.

"Need me to come along?" Jinx asked.

Oh, hell no. There was venom in her voice, revenge simmering just below the surface. She might not shoot Delilah, not yet, but that didn't mean I wanted us all to get together. No way.

"That's okay," I said, voice abnormally chipper. "We've got it. Talk to you soon. Okay, bye!"

I hung up and let out a shaky breath. Ceff shook his head and grinned.

"I know, I know, I'm not a good liar," I said, cheeks heating.

"The worst," he said. "Not that it was truly a lie. We do have this, as you say. It was smart to keep her away from the succubus."

"Far, far away," I said.

CHAPTER 23

I bit my lip and dialed Torn. I didn't want to interrupt him and Delilah in flagrante. My eyes had suffered enough.

"I texted Torn to meet us by the service entrance," I said, shoving the phone back in my pocket and facing Ceff. "Delilah can cover the front gate while we chat."

I crossed my fingers, hoping that Torn would know a way to get us to London and that he'd be willing to go to the trouble. For all I knew, he'd want to stick around the carnival and combine killing zombies with sexy times with Delilah. Either way, I needed a favor and it wasn't the kind of thing I could ask over the phone.

Thankfully, we made good time. That was partly due to the fact we were heading downhill, but we also didn't meet any trouble. Joysen Hill remained ominously quiet.

Torn quirked an eyebrow at our speedy arrival, but I shrugged.

"So, what is this all about, princess?" he asked. "Are we ready to fight more zombies? Preferably, something larger than a gerbil. I do have standards."

"Actually, that's why I'm here," I said.

A wide grin slid across Torn's face.

"We found a back door to the Necropolis," I said.

He flexed his claws, bouncing on the balls of his feet.

"Where?" he asked. "I imagine there are plenty of deadly things in a place called the Necopolis. This is going to be fun."

"That's the problem," I said. "The portal is in Highgate Cemetery, in London."

"Ah," he said, narrowing his eyes. "You want a favor."

"Think of it as a mutually beneficial arrangement," I said, spreading my hands wide.

"While I appreciate that attempt," he said with a wink. "That's not how this works. It's a matter of supply and demand, and my reputation. But good on you for becoming sneakier, princess. I like it."

"Before we discuss bargains, we deserve to know if a pathway exists," Ceff said. "Otherwise, we are wasting precious time."

If Torn wouldn't take us through the shadows to Highgate Cemetery, we were screwed. I'd considered our options, rolling the possibilities around in my head, on the way here. The only choices we had were the back door or the front door which was guarded by a mostly indestructible zombie dragon.

So, I forced myself to smile and negotiate with Torn.

"I can take us all to Highgate Cemetery, if you'll grant me a favor," he said.

"I'm going to regret this, aren't I?" I asked.

He shrugged gracefully and I resisted the urge to punch him in the face.

"Okay, I'll bite," I said.

He leered, but Ceff stepped between us, losing his last shred of self-restraint. My betrothed was a patient man, as was evidenced by him putting up with my never-ending stubbornness, but it had been a long day.

"What do you want, cat?" he asked through clenched teeth.

"I need something from a friend of yours," Torn said, head swiveling to face me.

That didn't sound too difficult. I should have known better.

"What is it that you need?" Ceff asked, suspicious.

"It's a mere trinket," Torn said, waving nonchalantly. "But one of my kittens is in a bit of a bind."

"And this trinket will help this cat sidhe?" I asked.

"Do this and I will take us through the shadows to the portal at Highgate Cemetery," he said.

It's not like we had much choice. No way was I getting in a flying tin can, and we needed to get to London asap.

"Fine," I said. "So, who is this supposed friend of mine?"

"Jenny Greenteeth," he said.

Mab's bones. I was almost willing to hitch a ride on a plane. Jenny Greenteeth was a water hag who lived in a nearby swamp on the edge of the marshes where the river merged with the harbor. It was a place of razor-sharp saw grass, bloodthirsty flies, and deadly quicksand.

"Sounds like fun," I said, voice thick with sarcasm. "You coming with?"

Jenny, all four of her personalities, lusted after Ceff. Knowing Torn, it was one of the perverse reasons why he'd chosen this task. I wasn't looking forward to paying Jenny a visit, but it might go better for my fiancé if he wasn't the only sexy man for the water hag to fixate on.

"I can't," Torn said, actual disappointment in his voice. "Sadly, the water hag and I have a complicated history. This isn't the first time she's had something I wanted. It's just the first time that I'm not fighting her for it."

Interesting. I knew that Jenny had spent some time at the Unseelie Court in my mother's inner circle. That hinted at her power, but it was hard to reconcile that the water hag I'd met had somehow bested Torn in a fight. I guess that meant I'd have to settle for solving one of Jenny's creepy riddles.

"I can hardly wait," I said.

CHAPTER 24

I was sorely tempted to make a pitstop at Eden Park before heading to the stagnant pond where Jenny Greenteeth lived. Marvin had saved my life the last time I went to the water hag for information.

"Is it wrong that I want Marvin as backup?" I asked.

On my last visit to the water hag, in my pig-headedness, I'd almost marched headlong into a watery grave. Marvin had stopped me, grabbed a piece of driftwood, and showed me the deadly truth. What had appeared to be solid ground, was in fact an interwoven web of floating moss, duckweed, lily pads, frog's-bit, covering a deadly pit filled with a hungry water hag and the bones of her victims, and, I now hoped, a bracelet.

"The young troll managed to turn the tide in your battle against the Pied Piper of Hamelin," Ceff said. "I would not mind his assistance with the water hag, especially if what you say of her…appetites are true."

I'm pretty sure Ceff wasn't talking about Jenny's hunger for the tender, bloated meat of those who drowned in the murky waters of her home. No, the thought of the water hag devouring human flesh and picking her teeth with the bones of unwary children made my stomach churn, but it was a different kind of hunger that set my beloved on edge.

Ceff had caught Jenny's eye when he'd been chained and dragged through the marshlands by his each uisge captors. The water hag referred to him as the "handsome kelpie man" and all her personalities had expressed a desire to ride him, in all of his forms, horse and man.

"Oh, trust me," I said. "It's true. Jenny Greenteeth has the hots for you."

In fact, promising to pass along that message was one of the reasons that Jenny allowed Marvin and I to escape. The water hag had wanted Ceffyl Dŵr to come visit. She was about to get her wish.

Ceff flinched, but I held up gloved hands, palms out.

"Don't shoot the messenger," I said, a grin tugging at my lips. "And you can't fault Jenny for having great taste."

Ceff shivered and shook his head.

"Forget that I broached the subject," he said, wearing a pained expression.

"Sure," I said.

I rolled my shoulders, but the tension remained. It would have been comforting to bring along backup, but everyone had their own responsibilities.

Even Marvin and Hob were busy guarding Eden Park from the zombie threat. The garden dwelling faeries needed their own hero and I had a feeling that Marvin had found his calling. The kid had grown into a man and he didn't shirk his duties. As Marvin had said, he'd protect them. He was their champion.

This job, to retrieve a jeweled bracelet from Jenny Greenteeth, was up to Ceff and I. Anything else was selfishness.

We walked in silence, both haunted by the fear of things to come.

CHAPTER 25

The marsh was unnaturally quiet here. We'd left the steady buzz of insects and the cry of seagulls behind.

"Is the water hag nearby?" Ceff asked, scanning the area warily.

I nodded, slowing and using caution as I placed my feet on the spongy ground. I wouldn't go rushing headlong onto the ill-perceived easier path, not again.

"I'd bet money on it," I said, pausing to search for landmarks. "Those vines look familiar and it's quiet as the grave in these trees."

Eerie laughter bubbled up from the water at our feet, and I had a distinct case of déjà vu. A slime-covered head rose to meet the pond scum-filled cackling. Faeries, the old ones especially, really do love a dramatic entrance. They're nearly as bad as vampires.

As the water hag broke through the pond's slimy surface, rust-colored water and green strings of algae dripped from her long, straggly hair. It hung in sickly clumps, exposing patches of corpse-gray skin that clung to her skull. Jenny's laughter trickled to an end as she laid eyes on me and someone just over my shoulder.

Her eyes widened and a fiendish grin spread across her face. Thin blue lips pulled back to bare crooked, overlapping, green teeth resembling a jumble of moss and lichen covered bones, not unlike the mass grave that likely lay at the bottom of her pool.

"Mab, darling!" Jenny Greenteeth exclaimed.

I staggered, head jerking as if I'd been slapped by an ogre. I spun on my heel, searching the marsh for the evil Unseelie Queen.

"That's not Mab, you ninny."

"Sure looks like her."

"This one's not nearly as pretty."

Ceff stiffened, but I stepped in front of him, toes of my boots at the edge of Jenny's slimy pond. This was no time for foolish pride. Ceff breathed heavy at my back, and I wondered for the hundredth time if I should have come alone.

The last time Ceff had been here, it was enslaved to the evil each uisge. It was a time of pain and torture for him, one of his worst memories. I should know. Whenever we touched, I relived his most traumatic moments.

But Ceff had insisted and, to be fair, I desperately wanted him at my back. I hadn't wanted to come alone, but maybe I should have brought Marvin, after all. I had to hope that Ceff, and Jenny's crush on him, would be the ace in the hole we needed to retrieve Torn's required bauble.

Not that I trusted Torn. I doubted that the bracelet was the mere trinket he claimed it to be. I pursed my lips.

If I was totally honest, I was still surprised that he'd required a price for the transaction of taking us through the shadows to London. Torn had been just as eager as the rest of us to go to the Necropolis, more so. But this was the faerie way. Our world seeks a balance, and this was the price we had to pay for travel to Highgate Cemetery.

"I'm not Mab," I said, taking a deep breath. "I'm her daughter."

I heard a sharp intake of breath at my back, but I kept my eyes forward. This was a gamble and I had no way of knowing how the water hag would react.

"The Queen of Air and Darkness had a babe?" Jenny asked.

"I'm always the last to know."

"She's not so special."

"Oooh, can we keep her?"

"You used to visit my mother's court," I said, trying to wrangle Jenny's attention and maybe, just maybe, infer a position of power and respect high enough to keep the water hag from deciding I'd make a great entrée.

"Mab was a brilliant rider," Jenny said.

"She had the best stables."

"So many monstrous creatures to ride."

"I can still taste their fear."

A grub-like tongue lashed out to lick blue lips and I fought down my revulsion. I hadn't wanted to shift Jenny's thoughts to riding. Hell no.

"I remember you," she said, eyes locking on Ceff.

"Handsome kelpie man."

"She did it."

"The wisp delivered our message."

Jenny leered, and I almost swore in frustration. There had to be a way to draw attention off Ceff. Too bad he chose that moment to step to my side in full view of the drooling water hag.

"I seek a boon, water hag," Ceff said.

His voice was steady, but I could see the slight trembling in his hands. Ceff might be a kelpie king, but he wasn't invincible and right now, this place and the memories it evoked was getting under his skin.

The surface of Jenny's watery pit rippled and quivered, her desire almost palpable. My beloved had just offered up a tasty morsel that she couldn't resist.

"What do you seek?" Jenny asked.

"What do you offer if you fail?"

"I do hope he fails."

"It's been so long since we rode a kelpie."

"We seek a bracelet lost here long ago," he said.

"And I offer a swim in your pond if we fail," I said.

Jenny's head swiveled and all eyes fell on me.

"Ivy," Ceff gasped.

I ignored him. I wasn't letting my betrothed offer himself to Jenny Greenteeth. Ceff was a king. He had responsibilities beyond Harborsmouth. If anyone deserved to go swim with the water hag, it was me. It was my bargain with Gaius that had us here in the first place.

"I am the daughter of your queen," I said. "I am an acceptable tribute."

Jenny pouted, sticking out her corpse-blue lower lip. I held my breath and waited. It was a damn good thing that I did.

I'd expected a riddle to solve or a game to play. Not for one hot second had I anticipated the vine lashing out, grabbing me by the booted ankle, and tossing me into the murky water.

Ceff's scream barely registered as my brain focused on survival. I thrashed, praying to Mab and Oberon and any human god that might listen to not let anything in this fetid cesspool trigger a psychic vision.

If that happened, I'd drown for sure. As it was, I had a fifty-fifty chance of fighting my way to the surface.

Right now, I wasn't even sure where the surface was. Pond scum and algae clung to my face and acrid water stung my eyes. I tried not to think of the reasons why the water was so foul. I had enough nightmares without thinking too hard about Jenny's lack of indoor plumbing.

Plus, I had no time for distractions. I was too busy trying to survive.

A hand clawed at me. I struggled, eyes opening in terror. But as frightening as my attacker was—a skeleton whose bones were covered in teeth marks—the hand didn't belong to the water hag. I'd escaped her clutches, but not for long.

Jenny dove, rushing toward me, but not before I saw the pile of bones littering the bottom of her pond. This wasn't just a collection of bones. It was a mass grave. And the killer responsible was heading straight for me with murderous intent.

I rolled, struggling to remain out of the water hag's reach. My eyes searched for a bone in a bone stack. I knew the odds, but I kept looking. The bracelet had to be here somewhere. It's not like Jenny had a storage unit. All her treasures were here for the taking, so long as she didn't kill me first.

There was also the small matter of drowning. My lungs burned and I knew that I had mere seconds before I was out of air. In fact, when I saw a sparkle, I thought it might be from oxygen deprivation. That's when I felt it, Ceff's magic.

A water bubble eased over my face, providing me with a gulp of much needed air. Ceff was water fae and his water magic was impressive. He might even have saved my life.

With renewed energy, I dove toward the murky bottom toward the gleam of treasure. I had to make this try count. I wouldn't get another chance.

Ceff wouldn't be coming to my rescue, not with air anyway. From the water churning above me, and the bodies thrashing closer to the surface, Ceff had jumped in to join the fight.

Jenny Greenteeth might be a powerful water hag who used to hang out with my mommy dearest, but Ceff was a kelpie king fighting for the woman he loved. My money was riding on my betrothed.

Not willing to waste the opportunity, and what I was desperately hoping wasn't his sacrifice, I grabbed a femur with gloved hands and dragged myself closer to something metallic gleaming in the spectral light.

Upon closer inspection, there were two items, jewelry sparkling from the hand and wrist at the end of a skeletal arm. Unfortunately, the arm was jammed inside a rib cage. I yanked hard, trying to pry the bones apart, but they wouldn't budge.

White dots appeared before my eyes, a sure sign that my body was oxygen starved. I should have kicked my way to the surface. It was the smart thing to do.

Nobody ever accused me of being sensible. I grinned, my lips still tight together, holding in the last bit of air. I pulled a dagger from my boot with fingers that were going stiff and numb. My movements were sluggish, but I couldn't give up now. I had to try.

I hacked and stabbed at one of the ribs with the dagger. The pointy blade wasn't the best tool for the job, but it was the best I had available in this quagmire. Leather straps are a nightmare underwater and the mechanism for my forearm sheaths was designed to work with gravity not gravy. The dagger would have to do.

I missed more than once, and some of my hits glanced away without any real impact, but the rib moved. The edges of my sight darkened, tunnel vision setting in. That was a bad sign. I knew it was, but I grabbed the rib and arm with both hands, my boots slipping along slimy, algae-covered bones, unable to find purchase.

The arm came free of the rib cage and I clutched it to me, hoping it wouldn't somehow touch skin. On the plus side, if I got caught in a nasty vision, it wouldn't last long. I was pretty sure I was dying.

But I didn't want to die here. The idea of my body being eaten by the water hag, my gnawed upon skeleton littering the murky bottom of Jenny Greenteeth's pond, was enough incentive for one final surge of adrenaline.

I swam for the surface, wondering detachedly where the water hag had gone. Then a horse or a man, dragged me onto the mossy embankment. The world spun a few times before I flopped onto my side and vomited up a few gallons of pond water.

A shadow fell over me and I snarled.

"Ivy, it's me," Ceff said.

I knelt, leaning back on my haunches, clutching something to my chest, blinking at Ceff.

"Are you all right?" he asked, worry etching his face.

I frowned, wondering what the dark, oily goop was on his cheek.

"Mmm hmm," I answered.

I was dazed, but alive.

"Is that a human arm?" he asked.

My chin dropped and I came face to arm with a skeleton. I dropped the bones, cold fear skittering up my spine. The fear cleared away the fog of confusion but did nothing for the dizziness that swarmed inside my skull like an angry hive of pixies.

"Um, yes," I said, biting my lip against the rising vertigo.

I took a deep breath and tried to focus on what was in front of me. A ring glittered on one of the skeleton's remaining bone fingers, but I was more interested with the sparkly bangle on its wrist.

"I think I found Torn's bracelet," I said.

I looked up at Ceff, but the triumphant smile froze on my face.

"You nearly drowned," Ceff said, the skin around his eyes tight with worry. "You...you could have died."

"Mmm," I muttered. "Don't need saving."

My point was weakened a tad by my body being wracked by another dry heave. I'm pretty sure I'd coughed out every ounce of pond water but try telling my stomach that.

"I am aware of who you are and what you are capable," he said. "You do not require saving, but I would aid you. If you let me."

I guess he had a point. I was cold and wet and miserable, and I could barely stand on my own.

Ceff's love came with no strings. He'd love me, support me, and follow me into the abyss—or in this case a water hag's foul pit—with zero guarantees, no bargains. He gave his love, and his support, freely. The more I learned about faeries, the more I realized just how rare our relationship was, especially among a culture that valued backstabbing and double-dealing.

And, yeah, I was babbling. In my mind. Probably not a good sign.

"Fine," I whispered.

Ceff slid an arm under mine and around my back, keeping me upright. This close, I could feel the tension in the rigid muscles. He was either scared or mad as hell. Maybe a bit of both.

I owed him an apology.

"That didn't really go the way I planned," I said. "I'm sorry."

"Are you saying that you had a plan?" he asked.

"Um, sort of?" I said. His gaze locked on mine and I winced. "Okay, not really. I thought it would be easy, ish. Solve a riddle. Try not to piss off the powerful faerie. The usual."

"The usual," he said, voice thick with emotion.

"Well, I mean, I thought I might have to protect your virtue," I said, hoping to lighten the mood. "Jenny kept looking at you like you were her own private ice cream cone."

Ceff didn't smile, but his face softened. He turned toward a heap of green and grey that I'd been trying to ignore. My mind was screaming that it was just a pile of fish, and frogs, and algae. Nothing to see here. Nothing at all.

"I had to kill her," he said, voice sad.

"I'm sorry," I said.

"The city is safer now," he said, shaking his head.

"It is," I said. "But Jenny was old. I hate what she did, but I kind of understand why she was the way she was. I'm sorry you had to take a life."

He glanced at me in wonder.

"It is hard to lose the old ones," he said. "I wasn't sure you would understand."

But I could feel it. The sorrow. A breeze stirred the copse of trees, wringing from the branches a sighing moan. I rubbed at my arms and shivered.

"Please, let me help you," Ceff said.

He wanted to help. He wanted to be included. He didn't want me leaving him to watch while I stepped off a cliff.

So, I let him help.

"I could use a ride," I said.

I was exhausted, my head was pounding, and I was sick of this swamp and all the sorrow it held. I'd been dreading the slog back to the Old Port Quarter. A ride would be nice.

"Tell me where to take you," he said.

Water streamed down my face, not all of it from Jenny's pond. Memories of the child-sized skeletons with their chewed upon bones kept bobbing to the surface.

I nodded, and Ceff knelt, shifting into a gorgeous, sleek grey stallion. I climbed onto his back, blinking back salty tears.

"The loft," I said.

I needed to hug my kid, now more than ever.

CHAPTER 26

I waved at Forneus, hurried through the apartment and snuck into the shower, Ceff right behind me, but my kid caught me on the way out. Sparky was going to be doubly excited when he saw that daddy was home too. My heart swelled and I smiled down at my kid's adorable, floppy ears and huge grin.

"Hey, pumpkin," I said.

"Pumplestiltskin!" Sparky squealed.

"We've been reading fairy tales," Forneus said.

"For real?" I asked.

"I could regal him with tales from Hell, if you prefer," he said.

"No, nope, fairy tales are great," I said. "So, where's Jinx?"

I looked around the apartment, but I didn't see my Rockabilly friend anywhere.

"I believe she is in your bedroom," he said. "Something about moldy dishes."

I shrugged with one arm and strode into my bedroom ready to face Jinx's wrath. I'd rather go fight the lich.

But I could hear the water running in the shower. Ceff needed a moment to recover from seeing me almost die, again, so this was as good a time as any to chat with Jinx about how I was a crappy roommate.

"Sorry," I said, rubbing the back of my neck.

"You know I could probably knit a sweater with the mold growing off these," Jinx said, holding up two coffee mugs.

"Please don't?" I said.

"Only if you stop leaving your dirty dishes around for Sparky to find," she said. "He got creative with finger painting the kitchen floor earlier. Fresh coffee would have only been messy. One of your science experiments spread artistically over the linoleum was revolting."

"I'll try not to leave dirty dishes where Sparky can find them in the future," I said.

I just hoped there was a future.

"You're getting sneaky with your wording," she said, a grin tugging at her lips.

"And you've been spending too much with a demon attorney," I said. "Forneus is teaching you all his tricks."

"Oh, hon, you have no idea," she said.

"Ew, anywho, since we're on the topic of deals and bargains," I said, dragging the conversation back to bargains and the hell away from Forneus' bedroom tricks. There wasn't enough brain bleach in the world for that conversation. "I have a favor to ask."

"Shoot," she said.

"I need you to stay here and watch Sparky until this is all over with," I said.

"Fine," she said.

Um, that was easy. Jinx lifted a hand, before I could interrupt.

"But only because if Brandy or someone like her comes back, I don't want them facing an overprotective gargoyle," she said.

She had a point. If we left Sparky with Humphrey, I had no doubt the gargoyle would do anything to protect our kid. I did, however, wonder if we'd have a building, or any remaining clients, to come home to. Gargoyles aren't known for their subtlety. They are quite literally heavy-handed.

"You have a point," I said. "So, um, if this all go sideways..."

"I'll be the best mama that kid every dreamed of having, except for you of course," she said.

I let out a breath I didn't even know I'd been holding.

"Thank you," I said.

"Listen," she said, fidgeting with her hair.

She was making me nervous.

"Do I want to?" I asked.

Jinx rolled her eyes so hard, they nearly popped out of her head.

"You can do this," she said. "You can do anything. I believe in you."

"Oh, um, thanks," I said, rubbing the back of my neck.

"I'm not done," she said.

"Sorry," I said. "Go on."

"You are strong and crazy and courageous, and I would follow you into a fiery pit of faerie scorpions," she said.

"Do faerie scorpions even exist?" I asked.

She'd been doing a lot of research amidst wedding planning. Maybe, she'd learned something I hadn't.

"I don't know," she said. "It was the scariest thing I could come up with on short notice."

"You've been watching too many nature documentaries," I said.

Sparky had graduated from cartoon marathons to watching educational shows. I knew way more than I cared to about sharks and dinosaurs.

"I know," she said. "The point is, I love you."

"Oh," I said. "I love you too."

We didn't hug. We didn't need to. Forneus, on the other hand, took a bit more time with the physical displays of affection. But he didn't delay too long. If I didn't know better, I'd say the demon was eager for our little road trip.

Ceff was right behind him, looking refreshed from his shower. He stopped to give Sparky a hug and a kiss on the forehead, and I wiped a gloved hand across my face. My promise to Gaius must be taking its toll. The fatigue was making my eyes water.

So, we set off to give Torn his Mab-be-damned bracelet and hit the road to London where, according to Forneus, there was a gate to the Necropolis. We'd enter the back door to the necromancer's realm, sneak in, and kill him and his zombies. Easy peasy.

CHAPTER 27

I'd thought that Jinx and Forneus had put on a
gruesome show with their farewell smooching, but they had
nothing on Delilah and Torn. I coughed, alerting the succubus
and cat sidhe to our approach, but that just seemed to fuel
their bumping and grinding.

If they kept this up, I might consider a vampire memory
wipe. I'm sure Gaius would be cool with that once I helped
solve this case. Right, and PDA is an Olympic sport.

My hand slid to the pocket that held two sealed bags. I'd
taken both the bracelet and the ring from the skeleton I'd
found in its watery grave. I'm not sure why I'd taken the ring,
but at the last second, I'd tossed it into a second evidence bag
and slid into my jacket pocket.

Who knows? It might come in handy. If nothing else, it
would make a nice gift for Hob. Hearth brownies love sparkly
things. So long as I didn't start calling the ring my precious, I
was pretty sure it was just a pretty trinket.

"Hey, Torn," I shouted. I lifted one of the bags, careful to
reassure myself that it was the one that contained the bracelet,
hefting its weight in my palm. "Catch!"

I tossed the bag, hoping it would smack Torn in the
head. I was sadly disappointed. Torn spun, hand snaking out to
rip the bag from the air with cat-like reflexes.

"We have fulfilled your bargain," Ceff said, striding up
to stand at my side.

I'd given him a moment to shift back into his manly
form. Not that he'd needed it. He'd shifted effortlessly, even
after maintaining a steady gallop while carrying me all the way
here.

We'd made Forneus run alongside us, which was petty
but also kind of hilarious. Not that the demon was winded. Far
from it. Forneus stood beside Ceff, looking dapper in his
meticulous suit. He hadn't even broke a sweat. Neither had
Ceff, but my betrothed was scowling. I'm pretty sure he wanted
to wring Torn's neck.

"I see that, fish breath," Torn said, turning over the bracelet in his hand.

He held it up to the light, jewels sparkling, before turning back to Delilah.

"Here you are, sweetness," Torn said, reaching for Delilah's arm and sliding the bracelet over her hand.

I tensed, body going rigid. I wasn't the only one. Ceff's anger was evident in the taught lines and corded muscles of his tanned arms and neck.

"You are gifting her with the treasure?" Ceff asked, rage simmering.

"Of course," Torn said with a feline shrug.

"What about the cat you mentioned?" I asked. "You made me believe it would help one of your people."

My vision clouded, and I let myself dream about stabbing him. It was a good dream.

"Would you have fetched it otherwise?" he asked.

The thing was, I would have. I needed to get answers for Gaius and save my city from a lich king and his vile creations. I couldn't do that without a trip to London. Torn had me over a barrel of pixies, but there was still one thing that I didn't understand.

"How did you lie?" I asked.

Faeries aren't supposed to be able to tell a bald-faced lie. Even Forneus raised an eyebrow at that.

"She has a point, cat," Ceff said. "How did you manage that?"

"Would you like to explain the nickname, kitten," Torn said, running his fingers down Delilah's arm, making her purr with delight. "Or shall I?"

Ew. Barf.

"No comment, princess?" he asked with a smirk. "Cat got your tongue?"

I shook my head. Tearing apart the fabric of reality, watching a cat sidhe fold shadows into origami, and be spit out into some foul alleyway in a foreign city was starting to sound better by the moment. Anything to escape this conversation.

"Can we get on with the warping of time and space?" I asked.

"Ivy is right," Ceff said. "We have a lich king to kill."

"We do indeed," Forneus said.

Flame danced in the demon's eyes, and I realized belatedly that I had no idea who had created the portal in Highgate Cemetery that we were now racing toward. I hoped that this trip wouldn't involve a baptism of fire or following a yellow brick road of sulfur. Not that I could turn back now.

Delilah pressed against Torn and licked him, like a cat if truth be told, then stepped away. The succubus was staying behind to guard the carnival grounds, thank Mab. That left me, Ceff, Torn, and Forneus for this adventure. I just hoped it turned out to be roundtrip.

CHAPTER 28

The journey through the shadows wasn't as bad as a trip to Mag Mell or Emain Eblach, thank Mab, but I still gasped for air as the world shifted and London rose up to meet my booted feet.

Torn cocked a smug eyebrow and sauntered along the overgrown path as if taunting me for my human frailty. Not that I was human, not anymore, but, unlike the cat sidhe lord, my body wasn't used to traveling through shadows and portals. Torn lifted his hands and spun in a circle. How he managed to do that with a swagger, I'll never know.

"Welcome to Highgate Cemetery," he said.

That drew my attention. He'd brought us directly to the cemetery? That was unusually considerate for Torn. Either he was getting soft, or he was really eager to battle the lich king and his zombies.

"Um, thanks," I said with a slow disbelieving shake of the head. "I expected to be dumped in an alley or something."

I'd braced myself for a dirty puddle, bags of garbage, maybe even some vomit. Torn had a bizarre sense of humor, usually at my expense.

"I could still do that, princess," he said with a rakish wink and a devilish grin. "If you prefer."

And there it was, the real Torn. No way was I letting him drop me in an alley now.

"Nope, this will do," I said, stepping onto the center of the leaf-strewn path before he tossed me into the shadows.

I scanned my surroundings, surprised at the profusion of nature here. When Forneus had informed us the back door to the Necropolis was in a London cemetery, I hadn't expected a riot of wildflowers, trees, and ivy. I turned in a slow circle, marveling at the beauty of the place.

The scent of warm earth, greenery, and rain-dampened stone and Portland cement filled me with a rare sense of peace. But it wasn't silent here. There wasn't the hushed quiet of a church. Instead, there was a surprising sense of joy and celebration. Birdsong rang out through the lush overgrowth, birds happily chirping, tittering, and singing to the dead.

The joyous singing was a poignant counterpoint to the loss and decay.

Vines snaked from leafy branches, reaching down to caress the headstones and funerary monuments below. Lush ivy, my namesake, swarmed over moss and lichen, swallowing the graves whole.

Ceff cleared his throat, reminding me that we weren't here to sightsee. I sighed and turned to Forneus. He'd spent time here in the late 19th century and he had knowledge of the gateway that led to the Necropolis. That qualified him as our guide.

"Which way to the portal?" I asked, wishing we weren't on a deadline.

I didn't want to leave.

There was something about this place that called to me, creating a sorrowful ache deep in my bones. It was all I could do not to reach out and lovingly stroke the nearest headstone. The urge was so diametrically opposed to my usual touch aversion that I had to wonder if the place was bespelled. Were these funereal gardens just enchanting or enchanted?

Had we walked into a magical trap?

"Much has changed since last I was here," Forneus said, narrow gaze probing the surrounding darkness.

He didn't seem enchanted, only circumspect. Night hadn't fully fallen, but there was a perpetual gloom here amidst the wild trees and overgrown greenery.

"But you know the way, right?" I asked.

"Please tell me we didn't waste a trip through the shadows," Torn said.

"Yes, of course," Forneus said stiffly. His head swiveled as he got his bearings. "The design has not changed, only the effects of time and neglect. It was quite fashionable in those days, you know."

"Fashionable?" I asked, hurrying to keep up as Forneus hastened up a winding path.

"Are we talking graverobbing?" Torn asked, eyes gleaming. "Resurrections? Vampire tea parties? Do tell."

"Nothing so gauche," Forneus said, leading us at a punishing pace.

If I didn't know better, I'd think he was trying to outrun the past.

"Cemeteries, especially the Magnificent Seven, served as an oasis of nature for the city's humans who lived in London's smog and smoke," Ceff said. "They became the place to be seen, in their day."

Dry branches crunched beneath my boots and I tried not to imagine they were bones. Pesky morbid imagination. Instead, I considered Ceff's past.

"I didn't know you'd ever been to London," I said.

"Swimming the Thames was something that foolish, thrill-seeking kelpies did when they grew weary of the world," he said with a shrug.

"I'm sorry," I said.

"I would not do it today," he said. "I have much to live for."

I was glad for that. I'm sure Ceff's dark period was due in large part to his sociopathic wife murdering his only sons. That was a deep wound that I hoped Sparky and I could someday heal.

"If you two are done being disgustingly emotional, it looks like we're here," Torn said.

He rolled his eyes, but his stance was alert and ready for a fight. I could see why. Forneus had come to an abrupt stop, hellfire flickering in his eyes as he looked out over a ring of sunken tombs.

Curved vaults lined the circular lower terrace, the tombs carved into the hillside. Towering above, in the ring's center, stood a majestic cedar tree.

"The Cedar of Lebanon," Forneus said, voice hushed and reverential.

CHAPTER 29

I'd seen Forneus shrug off holy water, so I was surprised when he winced, stepping gingerly as we began our descent to the ring of sunken tombs. Tendrils of smoke rose up beneath his feet as he made his way down each stone step. I had to wonder about the holiness of this place. And that wasn't the only magic active here.

"Once we reach the bottom," Forneus said, breath ragged. "Walk clockwise to the thirteenth vault, then widdershins around the entirety of the Circle of Lebanon before exiting through Egyptian Avenue."

"Like a magic padlock?" I asked.

"Precisely," he said, a weary grin tugging at his lips. "How perceptive."

"This design, the ring with the tree as the centerpiece," I said. "It's fairy-crafted, right?"

I may not know as much as the demon did about London funerary architecture and cemetery design, but I knew faeries.

"There is much power here, but yes," he said with a nod. "Faeries were the original architects of the gateway to the Necropolis."

"So, how do you know about it, demon," Torn asked, narrowing his eyes at Forneus.

"I told you," Forneus said, waving a gloved hand. "I had business here in the 1880s. My role, as is my damnable curse as solicitor to the fae, was to negotiate and settle a territorial dispute between the fetch and banshee clans, including multiple counts of alleged wrongful death portents."

Forneus took a few more steps before coming to a halt and mopping at his forehead with a lace-edged handkerchief.

"I was privy to all records in the fetch and banshee clans' possession regarding their legal rights to perform their duty of portending a person's impending demise," he said. "Those records dated back to the creation of this cemetery and the portal we now seek entry to."

I nodded.

"So, to answer your question, yes, faeries designed the gateway," he said, casting me a contemplative look. "Which might explain the profusion of weeds and vines since my last visit."

It was true. There was no arguing the ties between faerie magic and the natural world, or the fact that this place was wildly overgrown. The greenery was growing untamed, swallowing the monuments to the dead.

"Nature has a foothold here," Ceff said.

That was the understatement of the year. It was like the place had been sprinkled with the faerie equivalent of Miracle-Grow. And it wasn't just the weeds and vines. I lifted my chin, admiring the enormous cedar tree that rose from the circle's center.

"It's beautiful," I said, pointing at the regal tree. "But why cedar?"

I'd heard of oak, ash, and rowan being used for magical purposes, but not cedar.

"Cedar's for portals," Torn said with a shrug.

Forneus nodded his agreement.

"It's why we trick humans into placing cedar in their closets, attics, and under their beds," Forneus said.

"That's a joke, right?" I asked. "You're joking."

"I never jest about closets," he said.

Forneus might have said more, but with an eardrum-shattering wail, a banshee lunged from the dark alcove where she'd been hiding and hit the demon head on. The woman was skeletally emaciated beneath her tattered, lacy widow's weeds, but she rammed Forneus with the force of a linebacker.

"Hurry, to the thirteenth tomb," he shouted. "I am fine."

I ran, Ceff and Torn hard on my heels, but as we hurried on our final pass, hopefully unlocking the gateway hidden in the Egyptian Avenue, Forneus was still locked in combat with the banshee.

Torn dove into the fray, slashing at the banshee with his claws. She screamed and dropped to the ground before I had a clear opening to throw one of my knives.

"Go!" Forneus yelled. "I will hold them off and keep the way clear for your return."

"Them?" I asked.

The question was answered by a riot of blood curdling screams and wails. The sounds came from every direction.

"I'm not leaving you," I said. "Jinx would never forgive me if you died. It would put a major dent in her wedding plans."

He blanched but nodded.

"Perhaps, you are right," he said. "I would not wish to anger my beloved."

"So, any idea what's gotten into the banshees?" I asked.

"I don't think it's the banshees we need to be worried about, princess," Torn said.

I scanned the cemetery, searching the gloom for movement. It took a moment for my brain to process the horror before me. What I'd taken for moving shadows, the result of flickering, spectral candlelight, was in fact a mass of writhing corpses.

"Zombies," I gasped.

My eyes rounded and my heart skipped a beat as the dead clawed their way up from their graves.

"Do you hear that?" Ceff asked.

"I think we all hear that wailing, fish breath," Torn said.

"No, not the banshees," Ceff said.

Below the high-pitched scream boomed heavy thuds like the heartbeat of a giant.

"What is that?" I asked. "Please tell me it's not a zombie giant."

"That would be fun," Torn said, jumping atop a headstone and flexing his claws.

"I do believe that something is trying to escape that mausoleum," Forneus said, pointing at the stone vault.

Now that he mentioned it, I could feel the pounding in the soles of my feet. It was almost rhythmic, booming over-and-over again as something, a zombie presumably, beat its way free.

"Any idea who or what's entombed here?" I asked.

Cracks grew along the face of the vault like racing lines of quicksilver. I had to resist the urge to stomp on the stone, the old nursery rhyme like a mantra in the back of my mind. Step on a crack, break your mother's back. If only I could be so lucky.

I shook my head. Jenny Greenteeth's mutterings about Mab had shaken me more than I'd like to admit. But now was no time for mommy issues. We had an entire cemetery of corpses ready to lurch out and eat our brains, or faces, or whatever it is zombies do. Whatever that was, it couldn't be good.

"I have no idea, but if it keeps up that racket, it will wake Bob," Forneus said, eyeing the rows of family vaults.

I had no idea who Bob was, but it was clear from Forneus' worried expression that this Bob guy would wake up angry. I'd rather not be around when that happened.

"That sounds ominous," I muttered. "Okay, new plan. How about we run for the portal? We can still get there, right?"

"Yes," Forneus said, stumbling forward as a huge piece of stone hit his shoulder. "It will appear at the end of Egyptian Avenue. Run!"

That was all the incentive I needed. Calves burning, hands clenched around throwing knives, I ran.

Egyptian Avenue wasn't quite what I was expecting. Thankfully, there were no cursing mummies or angry sphinxes. There were, however, plenty of zombies.

Zombies burst from their coffins, clawing and climbing their way to their feet. From my estimation, we had about five seconds before the narrow street of the dead was overrun. Egyptian Avenue ran between more vaults, shadowed by a canopy of interwoven vines that perfumed the air with an herbal scent.

Sadly, it didn't cover the stench of rotting corpses. Zombies lurched and staggered, and I threw a dagger to sprout from the nearest dead man's brow. Sadly, it didn't slow him down. We needed to get the hell out of Highgate.

Ceff whinnied, apparently deciding his horse form was the wisest choice. Torn used my betrothed like a springboard, launching himself into the vines, grinning from ear to ear. I followed, leaping onto Ceff's back.

"Run!" I yelled, leaning forward, mouth close to his equine ear.

Ceff galloped while I kicked and batted away our decomposing enemy. More worrying were the cries and wails of banshees becoming closer by the second. I risked a look behind us where Forneus took up the rear. He sent a jet of hellfire down the narrow avenue, setting zombies, vines, and cobwebs aflame.

I had a feeling that Bob, whoever he was, was going to be pissed.

"Hurry!" Forneus shouted.

Torn swung from the overhead canopy, a blur of claws and blades, as he leapt ahead of us. We'd reached the end of the path which dead-ended in a ring of poppies, cedar, and ash. Inside the ring, magic swirled dizzyingly.

We'd found the portal.

Ceff knelt, and I slid off his back, blades at the ready, but Forneus waved us forward. This was it. I swallowed hard. Here we go.

Torn winked and sauntered through the portal without hesitation, an eager spring in his step. He was enjoying this. I, on the other hand, was more wary. There was a very real possibility that we might die in the Necropolis. I blanched, stepping over the threshold.

So long as we managed to stop the lich king and save Harborsmouth, I was okay with that. I would do anything for my city. I would die to protect Jinx, and to give Sparky a future. For all my flaws and all my mistakes, my intentions were just.

I was a hero.

CHAPTER 30

Here near the gateway, the Necropolis was like a mirror image of the London cemetery, except for the fact that it was devoid of color and covered in ash. So much ash, in fact, that it took me a moment to find my footing.

As I scanned the area for threats, I could see that the crypts, mausoleums, and headstones gave way to a barren landscape beyond. That wasteland was primarily fields of thick, grey ash dotted here and there with clusters of headstones like moldy bread. Sadly, the concentrations of graves weren't the only blight upon the Necropolis. Lines of zombies striped this realm like rotting, gangrenous welts.

"We should add this to the honeymoon wish list," I said, voice thick with sarcasm.

"Extremely romantic," Ceff said with a wink.

"It has its charms," Forneus said, eyeing the area with interest.

"You better be kidding," I said.

The demon raised one eyebrow, but said no more. Great. I'd been trying to break the tension that lay as heavy as the stench of death. If Forneus suggested the Necropolis to Jinx as a potential honeymoon spot, she'd have my head.

Speaking of heads, looming over the entire land like an evil shadow, was a throne of carved skulls. On that throne sat a figure in a dark, hooded cloak. It was hard to penetrate the stygian darkness within those folds of fabric, especially from this distance, but I was certain that this was our lich king. The glowing blue eyes and the skeletal hand that gripped the throne were a dead giveaway.

Torn hissed and I had to agree with him. The lich was evil. The raw power of this place, fueled by blood and death, made the very air thick and rancid. The sooner we took this guy down, the better.

I squinted, examining the lich in the distance, only to realize one more detail. On his head, beneath the hooded robes, sat a crown. Maybe he really was an ancient king. Not that it mattered. The man had performed vile blood rites, sacrifices, to raise the dead. And now he lured those animated corpses here to be drained of their residual magic, making the necromancer more powerful by the minute.

Forneus bit back a curse. Since he was a demon, there was a chance it was a real one.

"I know," I said, tamping down the urge to gag. "I feel it too."

Death magic slid past us like an oil slick, an oozing effluvium of blood and rot. It was the magic equivalent of swimming in sewage and I, for one, did not want to drown in it.

I reached for my magic, trembling with relief to find it ready and waiting. Like the blades strapped to my forearm, and hidden inside my boot, it was a comfort to know that traveling through the portal hadn't declawed me, so to speak. Having weapons meant that I had options. We had a chance to win this fight.

I strode forward, Ceff at my side. Torn paced in front of us, a tiger hunting its prey. Forneus watched the swirling portal at our backs. I glanced at my friends, Jinx's words echoing through my mind. We are stronger together.

I just hoped that she was right.

CHAPTER 31

There were two ways to destroy a lich; fire and decapitation. With my wisp magic capable of walls of flame and fireballs, and Forneus' demonic fire magic and his ability to summon hellfire, we'd thought that decision was simple. Torn and Ceff would help us fight through the zombies, clearing a path to the lich king and keeping the enemy distracted, while Forneus and I burned the necromancer to a cadaverous crisp.

Too bad our magic couldn't touch him.

It didn't keep us from trying. Even Ceff tried directing a small lasso of water at the lich king, willing to see if something other than fire magic would penetrate the lich's shields, but the creature batted it away as if it were a fly. No, less that. At least an insect can bite and sting. Our magic couldn't even do that.

Cold fingers of dread slid up my spine as I realized the horror of our situation. We might all die here in this wasteland shrine to death. All of us might be destined to become the lich king's playthings. Worse, we'd never get to see our loved ones again, but they might see us if the necromancer sent our zombified corpses after them.

I couldn't let that happen. There had to be a way to defeat the lich. I took a deep breath, surveying the surrounding deathscape, searching for a way to win this.

The Necropolis was a world of ash and bone, but for a moment, I caught a whiff of bitter marsh grass. A grin tugged at my lips and I gave in to the smile, baring my teeth. I had my machete strapped to the small of my back, hidden beneath my jacket. It had come in handy on our visit to see Jenny Greenteeth. I'd used the machete to hack away the overgrown grasses and vines that had blocked our path. The blade was deadly sharp. If I could get within reach of the lich king, it just might take off his head.

Decapitation it is. But how could I possibly make it through a horde of zombies?

I ran, sprinting around zombie ogres and hurtling over headstones, but even with faerie speed and agility and grim determination, I wasn't fast enough. The lich king was becoming more powerful by the second.

Magic swirled around the lich king in concentric rings of power, and diving through those rings were my friends. Ceff, Torn, and Forneus were going to get themselves killed.

The necromancer continued to repel water, fire, and hellfire. Our magic could not touch him, no matter how close we got. And the zombies were so thick here. We wouldn't break their line, not even with Torn leaping into their ranks, slashing and clawing with gleeful abandon.

Not in time.

I blinked, a wild idea working its way to the surface. There was an option I hadn't even considered, because I was still thinking like a human. In Harborsmouth, the human parts of the city anyway, that helped me blend in. But here in the hellscape of the Necropolis while facing down an immortal lich king, thinking like a human was a liability.

The answer was simple.

I hastily tore off my leather jacket, trying to ignore the unease churning in my gut. A cold sweat broke out all over my body, and it wasn't from my wisp magic. The last time I drew on that kind of power and unfurled my wings, I hurt a friend, badly. It was no surprise that I was hesitant, but this was the only way I could think of to save my friends. To save Ceff.

I closed my eyes and magic leapt to answer my call. It was surprisingly strong, stealing the breath from my lungs, but I ignored the drowning sensation, focusing and sending that magic between my shoulder blades.

That's when one more of the lich king's secrets became apparent, the clues sliding into place to form a complete picture. The necromancer had stolen a piece of Dunn's world, the land of the dead, a fact that I was sure the Celtic death god would be interested to hear.

But it got weirder. The lich had managed to stitch edges of his Necropolis to the human world, such as the gates we'd discovered in London and in Harborsmouth, as well as to Faerie. And with the constant pulling of those threads, he'd pulled those worlds closer together.

The lich king was a spider in the center of a web of power so great, I had no idea what would happen if we killed him. But we were about to find out.

I reached for Faerie, knowing now why my wisp power leapt like a rodeo horse, bucking and kicking to be free. This was wild magic, faerie magic, and it was mine.

Magic tore through me. Wings burst from my either side of my spine, slicing through my skin and tearing through my t-shirt, but not becoming tangled in it.

Zombies swarmed over my friends, overwhelming them with sheer numbers. As I leapt, Ceff went down under a sea of zombies.

Frantic, I took to the monochrome, ash-filled sky. I lost sight of Ceff, as even his head was swallowed beneath the lich king's army. Torn was still bobbing up for air, but even with the wicked gleam in his eyes, I could see he was tiring, making his way to the surface less often.

I pushed my wings, forcing my body to climb higher. From this vantage, I could see that Forneus was faring better than the others, keeping a small circle around himself burned clear with hellfire, but he wasn't making forward progress. He couldn't reach the lich king or our friends. There were too damned many of them, an endless raging sea of zombies, wave after wave of the animated dead.

I knew what I had to do. I just hoped I wasn't too late.

I circled around the throne looming over it all. The lich king appeared to be focused on my friend's struggles with his pet zombies, but I didn't expect that to last. In fact, I'm pretty sure my luck was about to take a dragon-sized turn for the worst.

I heard a flap of wings in the distance, and they certainly were not my own. No, these were like a clap of thunder on the horizon. The lich hadn't noticed me, not yet, but the zombie dragon had.

The dragon was far from my location, only now abandoning its post at the Harborsmouth gateway, but with those huge, leathery wings, it wouldn't take the creature long to close the distance. I was out of time.

I slid the machete from its holster where it had been strapped to my lower back, adjusting to its weight in my gloved hands. It wasn't as well balanced as my throwing knives, but it was sharp.

I reached a point over, and just behind, the lich king's shoulder and I shot toward him, flattening my wings as I dove. I needed speed, and whatever shred of luck I had left.

Wherever the lich king stabbed his skeletal finger, his army of zombies scuttled and stomped, trampling everything there to dust. Right now, he was pointing at my friends.

I gritted my teeth, gripped the machete so hard my knuckles hurt, and struck. The blade hit just below the lich king's chin. Pain jolted up my arms, but I didn't let go of the machete. That might have been a mistake.

My world spun, the jarring impact abruptly yanking me from the air. My wings tried to over-compensate and I felt a wrenching tear. But I held on to the machete, screaming as I kicked out at the throne, trying to gain the leverage I needed to sever through the ancient bone and steely tendons of the lich king's neck.

One booted foot caught on the necromancer's robes, and with a crack of my knee hitting stone, I toppled to the ground. I wasn't the only thing to topple.

I sucked air into bruised lungs, pawing at the ground, trying to crawl away from the necromancer's throne and put distance between me and the skull that rolled beside me.

It wasn't one of the moldering skulls that dotted the landscape, or a stone Memento Mori broken away from the throne. This skull was the head of our enemy. My mouth fell open and I stared incredulously.

The lich king was dead.

CHAPTER 32

You'd think that killing a lich king would grant me a breather. For just a moment, I thought it had. Weapons clattered to the ground, followed by the heavy, echoing thud of corpses. The zombies stopped fighting and dropped as if they were marionettes and the lich king's death had cut their strings.

I scanned the bizarre battleground, searching for my friends and for my beloved. Torn scowled, disappointed that the zombies had stopped fighting, and Forneus extinguished his ring of fire. They were safe.

I stumbled over the lich king's headless body toward where I'd last seen Ceff, halting breathless as he stood and turned to me. I felt a frisson of heat as our eyes met, but it didn't last. Good things never do.

A huge shadow fell over the battlefield, growing rapidly. My stomach clenched as realization dawned. Oh, Oberon's eyes on a stick.

"Run!" I screamed, waving my friends toward the vacated throne that loomed to my right. The throne was the only potential shelter and its location on the hill was, as far as I could tell, just outside the falling zombie dragon's trajectory. "Dragon!"

Torn quirked an eyebrow, and I heard a muttered curse. I ran, ignoring the searing pain in my bruised and battered wings as the air dragged at them like claws. I had to hope that my friends would follow.

Please, please, please don't take them from me. Not now.

A gust of hurricane force wind knocked me off my feet and I landed face down in a pile of ash. Too bad that wasn't the only ash problem.

I'm not sure what's the velocity of a falling zombie dragon, but when it hits an ash-dusted battlefield, it creates a mushroom cloud of cremated dead people. The world went dark, and I'm humble enough to admit, I might have passed out. Sucking in a lungful of corpse ash was more than my battle-weary, bargain exhausted mind could handle.

I came to, choking and coughing up soot and ash, but my friends were there. Ceff, Torn, and Forneus stood guard while I gasped for air and blinked gritty eyes.

They were alive.

I looked down at myself and back at my friends. We looked like chimney sweeps in a violent, twisted version of a Dickens story. I started to giggle.

"You have a strange sense of humor, princess," Torn said, shaking his head.

That only made me laugh harder. I bent over, hands on my knees, tears streaming muddy rivers down my cheeks.

"Did Miss Granger suffer a head injury?" Forneus asked.

I couldn't answer. I was too busy cackling like a Hollywood witch. I laughed out all the shock and horror, knowing that it was either succumb to convulsive laughter or uncontrollable sobbing.

The lich king was dead. The zombies were no longer a threat. My body was a tumultuous storm of unwarranted fear, terrible puns, and unspent adrenaline. I just might let myself laugh forever.

Too bad that's when pain flooded my body, my veins turning to rivers of agony.

CHAPTER 33

We'd survived. I'd stopped giggling, my face itchy with ash and tears, and all the aches and bruises from our battle with the lich king and his zombies were making themselves known.

"Mab's bones," I muttered.

I placed a gloved hand on my lower back, working out the kinks. At least, I tried to rub at my sore muscles, right up until I brushed past one of my injured wings.

"Oberon's eyes, I'm dying," I moaned.

"You're not dying, princess," Torn said. "But you do look terrible."

"Thanks a lot," I said, scowling.

"You will feel better once you are able to put your wings away," Ceff said. "And once we have returned home."

Home. That one word was like a shot of espresso. I couldn't wait to go home and hug my kid and take a hot shower. Maybe not in that order. I was covered in the ashes of dead people.

I shuddered, causing a new stab of pain to shoot through my wings.

"I just need to grab my things," I said.

I used my booted foot to sift through the ashes at the base of the throne, the place where I assume I'd dropped my machete. The moments of the lich king's decapitation and zombie dragon falling from the sky were a bit of a blur.

I was almost ready to give up the search for my blade when I checked behind the mammoth throne. There, in the shadow behind the towering carved skulls, was a creature huddled in chains.

I approached cautiously, my careful tiptoeing through the ashes attracting the attention of my companions.

"Is that a unicorn?" I asked.

"That is a night-mare," Torn said, tilting his head to the side. "Curious finding it here."

"He's not that bad," I said, hands on my hips. I probably looked like a nightmare about now too. "I think he's kind of cute."

The little horse-like creature was cute in a stabby sort of way. His fur was dark and wavy like a goat's, where it wasn't matted together, and his pointy horn twisted in a black and silver spiral, but his eyes were midnight blue and filled with stars. There were galaxies in those eyes.

I yawned, swaying on my feet.

"I don't mean he's a bad dream, or ugly, or a hot mess," Torn said, snapping me out of it. Oberon's eyes, I was tired. "A night-mare is a type of faerie."

"They're rare, thank Lucifer," Forneus said, fidgeting with his gloves.

The night-mare, a creature so monstrous it made a demon lord nervous, bleated pathetically and farted.

"What's wrong with her?" I asked.

"The lich king chained the night-mare here, enslaving it," Ceff said, the threat of violence in his voice. He was angry and deadly serious. "Then starved her, feeding it only the most rotten, vile, twisted parts of himself."

I swallowed hard. That didn't sound good.

"What do you mean?" I asked. "Like, he fed her literal chunks of lich corpse?"

No wonder the poor thing had indigestion.

"Night-mares feed on dreams and on the fear that those dreams inspire," Forneus said.

Torn waved a hand at the expanse of graves and mausoleums.

"The dead don't dream," he said.

"And?" I asked.

"Nightmares feed off dreams, good or bad," Ceff said.

"Mostly bad," Forneus muttered.

"But the only dreams here in the Necropolis were those of the lich king," Ceff said, ignoring Forneus.

I knelt down and smiled at the night-mare.

"Yeah, those would give me indigestion too, sweetie," I said, keeping my voice gentle.

She didn't flinch away or show her teeth. That was a good sign.

Leaning in for a closer look made the horrors of the creature's captivity even more apparent. Her fur was filthy and matted, and there were patches where her dark fur had started to fall out. My hands fisted at my sides and I fought down a shuddering sob.

"You are not thinking of bringing her home," Forneus said.

"She'll starve if we leave her here," I said.

"She smells like troll farts," Torn said, wrinkling his nose.

I shrugged. I was getting used to troll farts. That was the downside of pizza night with Marvin. Plus, I'd smelled worse. I lived with a baby demon who had a recent bout of noxious stomach distress due to a group of sorcerers. Sparky was better now, and we'd made the cloaked cabal pay, but I was a hero. I couldn't see someone in distress and just walk away.

"I'm not leaving her here to starve," I said.

I also wasn't going to leave her all alone. I took in a deep, shaky breath and crouched down to offer the night-mare my gloved hand. The fact that I was wearing my leather gloves meant that I should be protected from psychic visions, but I wasn't sure how a night-mare's magic worked. And, right now, it didn't matter.

I knew what it was like to be different. To be feared. To be lonely. So, I reached out and when she didn't shy away, I stroked her filthy, matted coat of fur.

"Who's a pretty, pretty girl?" I cooed.

And she was a pretty girl, because the most beautiful thing in that moment was the boundless love shining in her star-filled eyes.

"You know, the mare might be useful," Forneus said.

"How?" I asked, instantly suspicious.

"Night-mares can feed off any dreams, but their preferred food is their namesake," he said.

"She can give our enemies nightmares?" I asked.

I wasn't rescuing the little sweetheart just to turn her into a weapon. If she wanted to help, sure. But I wasn't using her like that. She'd been a slave long enough.

"She can draw away the horrors that haunt your friend's mind," Forneus said.

"Wait, what?" I asked.

Then his words sunk in. Kaye. My friend still lay comatose in a witch facility outside the city. I would do almost anything to help her regain consciousness. Could the night-mare draw away the painful memories and growing fear that kept Kaye trapped inside her own mind?

"If she can help us, I'll ask her nicely once she's healthy," I said. "After I take her home."

Ceff nodded.

"You would never have left her here and neither would I," he said, gaze shifting from Forneus to Torn as if itching for a fight.

I knew where the anger, and the protective instinct, came from. Ceff had been enslaved more than once. He also had a paternal streak a mile long.

"You're coming home with me little buddy," I said. "You got a name?"

The nightmare nudged the chain and I noticed a medallion similar to a pet ID tag hanging there. Etched into the medallion was a name.

"Fernvolg?" I asked.

The night-mare nodded her head with a whinny and a snort. She reminded me so much of Galliel it was making me homesick.

"Okay, Fernie," I said. "I'm sure we can find a nice place for you in the gardens with Marvin and Hob, or maybe in the church with Galliel. Until then, you can bunk in our office. We can use one of Sparky's old beds and some blankets for a nest and you can eat all the dreams you want."

Fernie nudged me with her nose. Oh yeah, I was already wrapped around her little hoof.

"Never a dull moment, princess," Torn said, a grin tugging at his lips.

"Lucifer save us all," Forneus muttered.

Ceff finished removing Fernvolg's chains and smiled. We'd solved the case, defeated the lich king, rescued an adorable night-mare, and maybe even found a cure for Kaye's condition. Not bad for a day's work.

"Let's go home," I said.

CHAPTER 34

The lich king was dead. It was time to go home, hug my kid, and sleep for a week. Too bad the Necropolis had other ideas.

"What the hell is that?" I asked, fingering my knives and shifting to a fighting stance. "Torn? You deal with shadows. Any ideas?"

Shadows slid down the bodies of the fallen zombies to pool on the ground. More shadows flowed from the outskirts of the Necropolis. They moved like living mercury, if mercury were made of darkness.

"Yes, cat lord, is this your handiwork?" Forneus asked, hellfire flickering behind narrowed eyes.

"No, by sweet Titania, this is not my work," Torn said, eyes wide as he stared incredulously at the writhing shadows. I believed him. For the first time since we'd met, Torn looked truly out of his depth. "I can coax and charm a shadow to let me pass, or to share its secrets, not command hundreds of the things. This...this isn't my doing."

"In all of my years, I've never seen such a thing," Forneus said, drawing a sword from his cane. As soon as he drew the blade, the cane disappeared. It was a neat trick.

The shadows increased their speed, slithering across the ground, heading toward the throne. Unfortunately, that meant they were also headed straight for us. I took an involuntarily step back, bile rising in my throat.

"I have," Ceff said, voice somber. "In the Forest of Torment and in the Unseelie Court."

It was true that shadows hadn't behaved normally in Faerie, especially in my mother's court. But as with most things related to Mab and to my uncle Kade, I'd tamped those memories down deep, wrapping them up and tying them up with a bow. It wasn't a healthy coping mechanism, especially now.

"Ceff's right," I said, taking another step back, praying to Oberon that I wouldn't trip and stumble into the lich king's throne or fall and drown under a sea of darkness.

"Interesting," Torn said. "The trees, and their shadows, in the Forest of Torment were hungry for blood. The shadows in the Unseelie Court were Mab's spies, passing along whispers to the queen and her court. What do these shadows desire do you think?"

"I don't care," I said, shaking my head. "So long as they stay away."

I did not want to be sucked into a shadow's vision. Was that even possible? Until now, I would have said a shadow peeling itself from their hosts and rushing toward me like some rabid monster while its brethren pooled and slid like hungry puddles of darkness wasn't possible, but that was happening all over the Necropolis. We were surrounded.

"That would seem unlikely, given the circumstances," Forneus said.

The shadows continued swarming, herding us closer to the throne. Scratch that. They were herding me closer to the throne. Somehow, I'd been cut off from my friends.

I shot a glance at Ceff, chest tightening. He was stabbing at the shadows with his trident, but the weapon had no lasting effect. The shadows continued to gain ground.

"Ivy!" he shouted, anguish in his voice.

Ceffyl Dwr, king of the kelpies, was caught against the shadow tide, trapped in an undertow. He knew better than I did that swimming against a riptide was futile, and deadly. But he wouldn't back down, not while someone he loved was in danger.

"I'm okay," I said, thankful that I could still tell a white lie.

Truth was, I was scared as hell. The shadows writhed at the base of the throne, as if a pack of barghests fought there, rolling and falling over each other, struggling for dominance. Not one shadow touched the throne, or me, not yet.

"What's happening?" I asked, voice a hushed whisper.

"Change," Torn said, tilting his head.

CHAPTER 35

Cold, malevolent shadows rushed me, invading body and mind. Their voices started as whispers, multiple conversations, slipping and sliding over each other, never coming into focus. Pressure built, but it didn't signal the usual headache or nausea. Magic filled the air, choking me, as the voices sent icy tendrils to invade my heart and mind.

The deeper they delved, the stronger their power, and the clearer their words.

"Claim us."

"Command us."

"Restore the throne."

"Command us, my Queen."

Queen? Mab's bloody bones, no.

But the shadows didn't fight fair. Like most things in my world, they sought out vulnerabilities, hitting me where my defenses were weakest. I could face death, but I wouldn't risk the lives of those I loved.

Shadows writhed, wrapping themselves into chains, dragging down my friends, dragging down my beloved, drowning them beneath the churning darkness. The shadows even swallowed the puff of ash as Ceff, Torn, Forneus, and Fernvolg hit the ground.

"Claim us."

"Command us."

"My Queen."

"My Queen. My Queen. My Queen."

It wasn't fair. But since when did Faerie play fair? Faerie was a dirty rotten opponent, but I could fight dirty too.

"Release them, or I'll kill myself," I said, holding my blade to my throat. I gasped, the truth of my words and the bargain of them hanging heavy in the air. "I'll do it."

"Release them?"

"Release my friends," I said.

"Friends?"

"RELEASE MY FRIENDS AND MY BETROTHED," I shouted.

"As you command."

"Command."

"As you command."

"Command."

"My Queen."

"No," I gasped, but it was too late.

I could feel the change. I'd made a mistake. The lich king had set a trap. It must have been the lich king, right? Although that didn't make sense. But I was drowning, suffocating. What mattered was that I'd tried to escape the trap and failed.

At least my friends would survive. Ceff would live. Maybe, he would make it home. Sparky wouldn't become an orphan again. The kid could still have a dad. My friends would take care of the city. They would keep it safe.

That was enough.

It had to be.

Pain coursed through my veins. Icy daggers lancing through me, the shadows and ice magic piercing my body and my mind to a heartbeat that resembled but wasn't mine. Somewhere deep inside my soul, I knew the source of that thrumming beat. It had been with me all along.

I couldn't fight it. I'd never escaped it. It was the heartbeat of Faerie, and I was tied to that realm with bone and blood. Shadow and ice. Air and darkness.

I wanted to die. I wanted the spell to end or end me. I wasn't so lucky.

The shadows and frost had been unbearable. I was nothing but pain and emptiness. I tried to reach for the hope that I'd always had, the human piece of me that still believed in true love and happily ever after. I shifted my focus and stretched mental fingers toward my heart, but it was encased in ice. The spark that was hope and love and goodness faded.

I thought that was the worst thing that could happen. My body was trapped and tortured. Everything that made me who I am was locked away, hidden so deep I couldn't be sure it truly existed at all. It couldn't possibly be worse.

That's when the vines sprung from the ground, from mausoleums, from every grave. The vines were made of ice, covered in thorns, and raced toward me with speed and purpose. I was their queen and so, I must be bound.

I screamed until the icy vines wrapped tightly around my mouth, thorns piercing my lips. I tried to turn, to see if my friends were still alive, but the vines held like iron chains. Vines wrapped around my forehead, twining and dancing in graceful pirouettes.

No.

I was a hero. Heroes save their friends. I wouldn't let my friends die.

I closed my eyes, reaching deep for the last vestiges of my wisp magic. It was Unseelie magic, but unlike the ice magic of my mother's court, this was the fire magic of my father's much smaller court. I pictured my father's solemn face and reached further.

There.

Hiding behind my frozen heart was a spark, a tiny glowing ball of wisp magic. It was depressingly small, but I didn't let that stop me. I reached for it, coaxed it, whispering promises that I wasn't sure I could keep. Lying to myself? I was damn good at that.

I was also good at saving the Mab-be-damned day despite terrible odds.

I sent the glowing wisp magic toward my heart. I shoved every bit of energy I had at it, demanding it to attack. I was attacking myself, but I didn't care. What kind of life would I have without my heart?

Heat and pain shot through my chest. Ice and fire burned, blackening the wall around my heart. With one final burst of magic, all that I had left, the ice inside my chest shattered. Cold light burst through the Necropolis and the vines and shadows retreated. I blinked rapidly, pulling a shuddering breath through lips that were no longer pierced with thorns.

My reflection glittered back at me in all directions from the many-faceted ice gems that covered the Necropolis. Every tomb, headstone, and mausoleum was encased and bejeweled, death enshrouded like a deadly geode.

The effect was dizzying, and I faltered. Any grace the ice magic had bestowed was lost as I stumbled, stomach churning as reality repositioned itself, and my role within it. I don't know how I knew that reality was shifting, only that there were endless things I had access to now, seas of truths floating and swimming within my blood. My stomach churned, but ice crept in further, holding my gorge from rising.

I wasn't thankful for the magic's assistance. I'd rather dump the contents of my stomach all over the sparkly throne. I prayed to Oberon and even Mab that Faerie would release me, would allow me to be almost human again.

But it was too late. The evidence of that shone with a cold brilliance that should have hurt to look at.

Upon my brow sat a crown.

It was beautiful and deadly. Thorns, roses, and blades that looked suspiciously similar to the ones strapped to my arms were spun together, a glittering ring of ice and shadow.

I pulled my gaze away, not willing to become ensnared by my reflection. There was something I needed to see with much greater urgency. I spun around, eyes searching the ground below the throne.

As I leapt forward, shadows and ice slid away from my friends. They looked shaken, but whole. They would survive.

The shadows and vines whispered as they retreated, dipping and bowing as they rushed away from the throne.

"All hail, Ivy the Queen of Air and Darkness."

"All hail, Ivy the Queen of the Winter Court."

"All hail, Ivy the Queen of the Unseelie."

My friends, every Unseelie fae, dropped to the floor. Only Forneus resisted, his head bowed and hands fisted at his sides rather than down on one knee. Torn and Ceff weren't so lucky. They were kneeling, their heads bowed, backs bent painfully.

An icy tear slid down my cheek, shattering as it hit the frost-covered stones at my feet.

"No," I choked, sobs breaking from my chest and tearing from a throat gone cold and raw. "No."

I ran to my friends.

"This can't be happening," I muttered.

I dropped gracelessly to the ground, lifting Ceff's chin. I didn't care that at some point my gloves had burned away. I touched his face, the skin scalding beneath my fingers. I didn't pull away, even when the tips of my fingers started to blister.

"I love you," I said.

His body was rigid and unresponsive, but his eyes were fierce. My Ceff was in there. He'd fought captivity before—first with the each uisge and more recently with the Wild Hunt—he would survive. He would come back to me.

"I love you," I said. "I don't want this crown. I don't want this power. I just want you."

More tears slid down my cheek. Were they less frozen now?

"I love you," I said. "I will never give up on us. Never."

Ice slid from my chest, painful icy spikes dragged through organs, bone, and flesh, but the cold retreated. It didn't go far. The magic never fully leaving me, but it lessened.

More importantly, my friends were free. Ceff reached for me, wrapping me in his arms.

My face was wet. I wasn't sure if it from my tears, which had returned to the messy, hot normal kind, or from my melting crown. Regardless, I could still feel the weight of the crown whether it had melted or not.

"Is everyone okay?" I asked, voice little more than a raspy, rattling croak as my vocal cords rediscovered the reality of flesh.

"Never better, princess," Torn said.

"I will endure," Forneus said, dusting off his suit and looking around for his blade.

I was pretty sure that Faerie, or its shadow and ice minions, had stolen the sword. Hopefully, Forneus could magic himself a new one.

"Ceff?" I asked, running a hand down his face.

My eyes widened in wonder. That was new. We couldn't usually touch without a vision. I'd always thought of that as a burden, or at least an inconvenience, but right now it was like a wall between us, shutting me out.

"I am well, so long as you are unharmed," he said, turning his head to press his lips to my palm.

"Princess?" Torn asked.

Forneus coughed.

"Perhaps, Miss Granger would like to retrieve her clothes," he said.

I blinked. My clothes? I looked down, belatedly realizing that my gloves weren't the only things to burn away during my transformation.

"Oberon's eyes," I muttered.

"Here," Ceff said, pulling his shirt over his head and handing it to me.

I frowned. Old habits die hard, but he was right. I'd touched his skin without a vision. His shirt was probably safe. And it's not like I was touching anything belonging to Torn or Forneus.

Fernie whinnied, nosing something half-buried in ash. No way. She'd found my leather jacket.

I shivered and put on Ceff's shirt, pulling my filthy jacket on over it. I glanced down, knobby knees peeking out from below the hem, and smiled. I looked like a kid, not a queen.

Not looking like a queen suited me just fine. Not being one would suit be even better, but that was a problem for another day. Right now, I wanted to crank the heat, crawl into bed, and sleep for a week.

"Let's go home," I said.

CHAPTER 36

I was cold and grouchy and in no mood for zombie hijinks. Thankfully, the zombies on the other side of the portal had become lifeless with the lich king's death, just as the ones had in the Necropolis. That's where our luck ran out.

Highgate Cemetery was hauntingly beautiful from our vantage as we emerged from the portal, traversing from the Necropolis, to stand at the entrance to Egyptian Avenue. We'd left destruction in our wake, but the stone vaults seemed to glow prettily in the gathering twilight.

For a moment, looking up through the canopy of vines to the majestic cedar framed by the archway, I wondered if Jinx would agree to holding the wedding here. A bouquet there, a ribbon here, and it would be a fitting place to exchange vows that were meant to last an eternity.

Well, it was almost perfect. I stepped over a fallen corpse. We'd have to do something about the zombies. I didn't think they added to a festive wedding atmosphere.

Something hissed to my right, and I jumped, staggering as my boot caught on a rotting shroud.

"This is unfortunate," Forneus said with a sulfurous sigh.

Okay, I had wrenched my hip, but I didn't know why he sounded so irritable. Maybe, he was suffering from low blood sugar. I couldn't even remember the last time I ate.

He waved his cane in front of my face and I glared over my shoulder. But Forneus was a few feet away, and he had his cane at his side. What the hell?

The thick, black thing in front of me lashed out and I stumbled back, right into the rotting corpse. If I survived this, I'd see if Fernie could eat my nightmares. Because, hoo-boy, this was going to create a doozy.

"You just had to wake up, Bob," Forneus said.

Bob was an orb variety of spider-fae who was currently waving his legs and mandibles at me threateningly. I got the message, but apparently, scurrying blindly backward over a pile of corpses isn't my best skill.

"Sometime this century, princess," Torn said.

I stumbled to my feet, and hurriedly lurched over the bodies. Bob wasted no time. Long, spindly black legs reached out and dragged a corpse into a nearby vault.

"What is he doing?" I whispered shakily.

"His job," Torn said.

My head pounded and my wings throbbed, and I had no idea what Torn was talking about. Bob continued to drag the fallen zombies back to their coffins while I stood as if rooted to the pathway.

"Is he going to eat them?" I asked.

Torn laughed and Fernie snorted, pawing at the ground. A grin tugged at Ceff's lips, but he gestured to Forneus.

"No, Miss Granger," Forneus said, letting out an exasperated sigh. "Bob is the caretaker."

"Oh," I said.

Torn's laughter still rang in my ears as the cat sidhe tugged at a shadow, stretching and folding the darkness into a pathway, taking us home. It was about time. I'd had it with liches, and zombies, and spider-fae caretakers.

CHAPTER 37

Standing in my bedroom, staring at the mundane normalcy of my unmade bed and laundry-strewn floor, drove home the fact that I was no longer normal. Normal-ish. I've never truly been normal.

I started having psychic visions when I was a kid. Not long after the psychometry kicked in, my second sight reared its monstrously ugly head. Much more recently, my wisp powers emerged, showing what my father's geas had hid all along, the immutable truth that I had never really been human at all.

You'd think I'd get used to change by now, especially the kind of change that left me fundamentally different than I'd been when I woke up that morning. But the fact of what had happened to me in the Necropolis sat like a lifeless, frozen weight inside my chest.

Did I even still have a flesh and blood heart?

That question was answered as soon as Ceff entered the room.

"How are you faring?" he asked.

"I'm still cold," I said, forcing a brittle smile.

I looked away, toeing a laundry basket. I was so, so cold. It's a miracle that my teeth weren't chattering. Maybe, if I bundled myself in every sweater I owned, I might feel more like me again.

"Look at me," he said softly.

My chin lifted of its own accord. Ceff was smiling. His smile was my undoing.

"It sounds as though you are in need warming up," he said, nodding his head sagely.

He closed the space between us, swallowing that distance in the blink of an eye. He reached for my face, rubbing a thumb along my chin. I hesitated, waiting for a vision to come. When nothing happened, nothing psychic anyway, I leaned into his palm, luxuriating in his warmth.

"You're probably right, but what do you think will do the trick for a case of Faerie-induced hypothermia?" I asked, meeting his heated gaze. "Coffee? A hot shower?"

"I can think of better ways to warm up," he said.

My stomach tightened. I barely understood his words, or the emotions that crossed his face, when he stepped away.

"This changes things," he said.

I froze, alarm rocketing through me.

"We'll have to redo our marriage contracts," he said.

Oh, right. Our contracts were for a kelpie king marrying a wisp princess, not whatever I was now. Necropolis queen? Unseelie queen? Queen of Air and Darkness? But it sounded like Ceff still wanted to marry me. I held onto that.

"We'll have to hire Forneus to make the changes," I said, frowning.

"I am more concerned with the added months of paperwork," he said.

"He'll probably charge extra," I said.

I groaned, but Ceff covered my mouth with his, my groan ending in a lustful moan.

"I am not happy about the delay," Ceff said, pulling away to look into my eyes. "I want to be your husband. I do not wish to wait."

"Well, you could get on with your husbandly duties early," I said, a grin tugging at my lips.

"What do you have in mind?" he asked. "I take my duties very seriously."

"Everything," I said.

CHAPTER 38

You hear about afterglow, but for me it was literal. It took a great deal of restraint to pull away from Ceff, drag myself out of bed, and tamp down the brightly glowing wisp magic that joy and passion had drawn to the surface. I didn't mind the world knowing that I was happy, but going around shining like a lighthouse beacon would cause trouble.

For all my royal heritage, I couldn't break the First Law. A crown may sit on my head, but some rules weren't meant to be broken. At least, that was the logic I was going with for now. I needed hard facts about Faerie, about our laws, our relationship with the human realm, and about what it meant to be a high queen. Too bad Faerie hoarded its secrets like a dragon hoards treasure. It would take time to pry away those secrets. For now, it would be best to keep my head down and stay out of trouble.

That was asking a lot.

"You are not going out like that," Jinx said, waving a finger at my face.

"Like what?" I asked, grinning from ear to ear. "Happy."

"I'll comment on that later miss fireworks and snowflakes," she said, wagging her eyebrows at me. "I meant the glowing eyes."

"Oh," I said, touching my face with gloved hands. "Thanks."

I closed my eyes, focusing on my wisp magic, and dragged it down beneath my glamour.

"Better," she said with a nod. She slid a mug of coffee across the counter. "Here, drink this."

"I am sure that Miss Granger needs it," Forneus said, emerging from Jinx's bedroom. He strode over and encircled Jinx from behind. "That was quite a spectacle you put on last night. It must have been…tiring."

Forneus stared across the breakfast counter at me and I stuck out my tongue. Then their words sunk in. The coffee churned in my stomach and I pushed the mug away.

"That wasn't just a bunch of lame inuendo, was it?" I asked.

"Dude, my inuendoes are never lame," Jinx, forced lightness in her voice.

"What did I do?" I asked, voice hushed.

Someone had sucked all the air from the room. It was only when Ceff strode out of the bedroom, blinking drowsily and smiling knowingly, that I breathed normally.

"I'm guessing this is about last night?" he asked, looking between us. "One moment. I believe I need to be fully caffeinated before we discuss Ivy pulling Faerie into our bedroom."

"It was...cool?" Jinx said, not convincing anyone.

"You have got to be kidding," I said. "That wasn't, I didn't..."

"I would not jest about what happens in our bedchamber," Ceff said.

"No, I know that," I said. "It's just, can someone tell me what's going on? I mean, it's not unusual for there to be, um, side effects from our wisp magic and water magic, um, combining."

Mab's bones, this was awkward. I'd rather be discussing lich kings than my sex life. How was this even a thing that was happening?

"Someone needs to put her out of her misery," Forneus said. "Allow me."

Jinx held up a hand, cutting off whatever he was going to say next. She looked at me, eyes softening.

"Ignore them," she said. "Pretend it's just you and me."

"Um, okay," I said, fidgeting on the bar stool. I took a swig of coffee and focused on Jinx. "What's up?"

"It's more like what was in our apartment," she said. "You made it snow."

"There was also quite a spectacular light show," Forneus said.

I rubbed a hand over my face. I needed a moment without everyone staring at me and talking about my personal life. If Jinx and Ceff were going along with this, and I wasn't being punked, then they were concerned. There was a problem here. I just had to parse it out and deal with it.

"Okay, the snow is new, but I'm not sure why we're all standing here talking about this before I've even had a decent cup of coffee," I said. "We don't usually do this unless there's major trouble or one of the kids are sick. Sparky isn't sick, is he?"

It had been late when we returned from London and we'd had calls to make and showers to take. Ceff, Forneus, and I had been covered in corpse ash. While they fought for the shower, my head pounding, I'd wasted no time calling Gaius, letting him know I solved the case, and getting out from under our bargain. We'd decided not to wake up Sparky. Had that been a mistake?

"Relax, Sparky is fine," Ceff said, putting an arm around me and pulling me close. "This is about you and your magic, and Faerie's claim on you."

"That doesn't sound ominous or anything," I muttered.

But relief filled me. Sparky was okay. The kids, as I tended to think of my many wards, were safe.

"We should start at the beginning," Forneus said.

"Please don't," I said, waving my hand. Whatever they were worried about, I didn't have an eternity to listen to a longwinded immortal demon. "Just cut to the chase. It snowed and that means?"

"That means you have some cool new powers," Jinx said. She drew herself up, shoulders back, and pantomimed holding a microphone. "And with great power comes..."

"Stop," I said, jumping off the barstool and glancing wildly at my friends. "I don't want great power."

"That is not up to you," Forneus said.

"It's part of the gig," Jinx said. "At least, that's what we know from a few hours of research. The two of us have been up all night going over what happened and what it means."

Jinx and Forneus had stayed up doing research, on me? And what was this gig she was talking about?

"What gig?" I asked, throwing gloved hands in the air.

"Becoming queen," Ceff said.

"As in, the kelpie king's wife?" I asked.

But I knew that's not what he meant. I already felt it deep in my bones.

"The Queen of Air and Darkness," he said, bowing his head slightly. "Queen of the Unseelie Court."

"No," I said, shaking my head. "That's not possible. I'm no..."

Queen.

I choked on the last word and dropped to my knees. Crap. I'd tried to tell a lie and my fae blood smacked me with the truth. It was a painful wakeup call.

"I don't want this," I said.

"I know," Ceff said, reaching out and sliding my hair behind my ear.

My eyes widened. His fingers touched my skin, but there was no vision. In fact, there'd been no visions in our bedroom last night either. I'd been so focused on being alive, coming home and being with the man I loved, that I hadn't even remarked on it.

That wasn't like me. I'm not sure what scared me more, the lack of visions or the fact that I hadn't made note of such a significant detail. I was a detective and a hero of the city. Details were my job. They made the difference between solving a case or winding up dead.

"How did it happen?" I asked.

There was no sense letting fear take over, or in lying to myself that I wasn't changed. The best thing I could do right now was treat this like any other case. Gather intel. Focus on the facts. Come up with a Mab-be-damned solution.

"Like I said, we must go back to the beginning," Forneus said. "Or, at least, the triggering event. From what we know, the lich king used his sorcery to create a pocket dimension, pulling a piece of Donn's domain into a bubble of reality and tethering it to the human realm."

"The Necropolis," I said, nodding. "That was one of our theories about the lich king and his kingdom. But he created the Necropolis ages ago, right? It's been tethered to Highgate Cemetery for at least a century, if the door existed when you were last there in the 1880's."

Good. Facts, theories. Working through the details that build a case and taking down the bad guy. This was my normal. I could do this.

"It's not just a theory, Ivy," Jinx said, leaning forward and speaking rapidly. "Donn came here. For real. And you were right. He totally looks like Santa Claus."

Forneus winced.

"I do not think the death god would approve of that comparison," he said.

"What did he want?" I asked.

"Was he alone?" Ceff asked.

Our questions were nearly in unison, the possible answers both as deadly. If Donn got pissed or if he brought along his girlfriend, we were all screwed.

"The Morrigan was not with him," Forneus said. "But she was mentioned. He warned us that war was on the horizon."

"And war is the Morrigan's bailiwick," Ceff said.

"Right, I take it that warning wasn't his reason to come here," I said. "It's not new information."

"Super weird to hear Santa Claus warning about the apocalypse though," Jinx said.

"Donn confirmed what we already suspected about the Necropolis," Forneus said. "The lich king created his kingdom by stealing small pieces of Tech Duinn and tying it to the mortal realm. More recently, he picked at the fabric of Tech Duinn's ties with Faerie, managing to create a small, temporary door through which he stole the night-mare."

"Poor, Fernie," Jinx whispered. "That must have been terrifying."

I was glad that Jinx seemed to like Fernie and had gone along with letting the night-mare spend the night in our office. I really did have the best friend ever.

"Unfortunately, this destabilized each of these realities," Forneus said.

Crap.

"He created weak spots," I said.

I could feel the truth of my words. I didn't need his confirmation, though I got it.

Forneus nodded and Ceff frowned.

"The king and queens left their thrones and closed all of the doors to Faerie," Ceff said. "But Faerie doesn't like to be caged, and it will always seek balance."

"So Faerie is like a cat," Jinx said. "If you close a door, it'll meow until you open it, or find another way through. Or barf on your pillow."

"That is an apt description," Forneus said.

"And super gross," I said. "Thanks for the visual."

"Any time," Jinx said with a wink.

I don't know how she does it, but my best friend had made me smile in the midst of another major crisis. Ceff was my rock, but Jinx was my heart.

"Would this have anything to do with how I managed to shift ley lines around?" I asked. "When Gaius threatened me in our office, I swear that when I reached for a ley line, they moved. I didn't think that was possible."

"Anything is possible when talking about the fate of Faerie," Ceff said. "Mab and Oberon and Titania left Faerie deeply wounded."

"But wounds heal," I said.

"Eventually," he said with a nod. "Faerie is a survivor."

"And an opportunist," Forneus said. "You've been drawing power to you, from the ley lines and, if I'm not mistaken, directly from Faerie. You, a direct descendent of Mab, are changing the connections of the human world to the faerie worlds. Your very existence has the potential to alter reality."

I gasped and the foot I'd been swinging went still.

"Faerie always finds a way," I said.

CHAPTER 39

"H ey, you okay?" Jinx asked.

"Something's been bothering me about this case, about the lich king," I said, running a gloved hand through my hair.

"Want to talk it out?" she asked.

I closed my eyes but nodded. Maybe, if I was lucky, that would help. I'd been working through a brain fog lately, fragments of truth swirling through that fog like glitter in a tornado.

Grief is like a concussion.

I'd read that when doing an internet search after Kaye went into the hospital, after my dad left, and after the magical doctors, it felt weird calling them witch doctors, called and told me that Kaye had fallen into a coma-like sleep and might not wake up again, ever. Search engines aren't great at answering the question of how long is normal to grieve the loss of a father who's still alive but has to leave to save your life, or the loss of your friend who is in a coma after you fought each other with magic. But in my search for answers, I did find one line that resonated with me and my pain.

Grief is like a concussion.

It explained the headaches, loss of appetite, and lack of focus. It gave me a scientific medical diagnosis to latch onto when I felt betrayed by magic.

But a concussion didn't explain the dredging up of old hurts. Instead of focusing on cases, I relived the feelings of abandonment from my father leaving, not once but twice. Grief is like a concussion, but it was more. Grief made me think about the betrayals by my biological mother.

Mab had made me think I was responsible for unleashing the Wild Hunt on my city when in truth that was a calculated attack that she had set in motion.

And, like that, a clear understanding of what had happened snapped into place.

"I've been wondering what motivated the lich king to come here to Harborsmouth," I said, opening my eyes. "Why here? Why now?"

"The ley lines?" Jinx asked.

I shook my head.

"I assumed it was the nexus of ley lines, or the power vacuum that Kaye and the glaistig left behind," I said. "But my gut never bought that theory. Something about it never felt quite right."

"What is your gut telling you now?" she asked.

"That this all ties back to Mab," I said.

Jinx's eyes widened and she glanced around the room, noting the exits. It was a good instinct. My bio mom was the original Queen of Air and Darkness. No matter how much Faerie wanted me on the Unseelie throne, I'm pretty sure Mab could still squash me like a bug.

"I hate your gut," Jinx whispered.

"Me too," I said. "But think about it. What if the lich king had been another one of Mab's puppets, little more than a plaything who could raise the dead."

"Creating minions to entertain her with, like the huntsman," she said.

"Exactly," I said.

"Okay, it fits her twisty murdery style, but why send the lich king?" she asked. "Why would she want Faerie to claim you? Why would she want you on her throne?"

"I don't know," I said. "But I have a feeling that I better find out."

CHAPTER 40

Reality, and Faerie's connections to reality, were changing. I didn't like the sound of that. Even worse was the implication that I might be the nexus for such change. Add in the meddling of my twisted sociopathic bio mom who liked to throw her toy monsters at me, and things went from bad to intolerably horrific.

My greatest fear, the one that kept me up at night, wasn't losing myself to a vision. That's the lie I told myself, but, deep down, it didn't track. The thing I'd always feared most wasn't the danger that stuck to me like congealing ghoul guts, it was the risk that danger presented to the people I loved.

I hitched the duffel bag over my shoulder and took a last look at our building. My home.

Sneaking out while Jinx was at work and sending her a vague text message about visiting Kaye was a betrayal, but the alternative might be so much worse. If my very existence altered the fabric of our world, drawing the monsters to me like a bugbear to a honeypot, didn't I have a responsibility to leave Harborsmouth, and my friends, behind?

"You really are your father's daughter," Torn said, slipping silently out of the shadows.

He shook his head with a weary sigh that held a heavy sadness I rarely associated with the usually flippant cat sidhe lord.

"What are you talking about?" I asked, wiping an arm across my face.

I frowned at my wet sleeve, wondering when I'd started crying. Judging by the light reflected from those tears, my skin had also started to glow. That was especially troubling. My control rarely slipped these days, not after my time in the wisp court training at the hands of my uncle Kade. Thoughts of my uncle only deepened my frown.

"You're leaving," Torn said.

"N-n-n..ng," I stuttered.

I growled in frustration, unable to deny it. I couldn't lie. I was too fae now. That was one more reminder of how much had changed. My hands fisted at my sides and I lifted my chin, head shooting up to meet Torn's gaze. He leaned against the wall, adopting his regular casual, carefree pose, but the tightness around his eyes spoke volumes.

"It won't help," he said. His scarred ears, what was left of them, flattened against his head and anger flashed briefly across his face. "Your situation isn't like Willem's. You haven't been cursed to carry a piece of Hell, an ember from The Pit, that brings destruction in its wake."

"I'm...I'm changing things," I said, waving a gloved hand at the rainbow-hued shimmer that covered the lamppost on the corner like unicorn snot.

Seeing that shimmer, and patches of unseasonal frost, out our window this morning was part of what prompted my decision to leave. I'd been home for a week now, and every day the city seemed to shift a little closer to Faerie.

"Change isn't always bad, princess," Torn said.

"Me being here could hurt this city, harm my friends," I said.

"It could," he said. "Or maybe, just maybe, you being here will save us all."

CHAPTER 41

I went back inside and got to work. There were still things I could do to help those I loved. It wasn't fair to leave it up to my friends to sort out. So long as I was doing more good than harm, I'd stay.

When had Torn become so damn smart?

I tossed the duffel onto the floor of my room and grabbed a protein bar for the road. What I had planned would probably take a while, if it worked at all. As with most things in life, there are no guarantees.

I left the loft again, taking the stairs two a time. Funny how hope has a way of putting a bounce in your step. Not that I was fooling myself that everything would turn out fine. I knew that staying here came with risks, and what I was about to do was dangerous, not just to me but also to a dear friend.

I breezed into Private Eye and set a cup of coffee on Jinx's desk. She looked up, her perfectly lined eyebrows raised.

"What's this for?" she asked. "And why aren't you at the asylum?"

I snorted and she rolled her eyes.

"You know what I mean," she said. "I thought you already left to visit Kaye and bring her some clothes."

"If what I'm about to do works, she won't need another overnight bag," I said.

"You're bringing Fernie to see her now?" she asked.

Jinx bit her lip, but I nodded.

"I think it's worth a shot," I said. "And worth the risk. Arachne's mother asked her entire coven to try healing Kaye and it didn't work. The Circle's verdict was that there was a blockage, like mental scar tissue, from too much trauma."

"Layers and layers of pain and guilt and loss," Jinx said, shaking her head. "She may not have liked me, and I was never her biggest fan, but nobody deserves that. And she was your friend."

"And a hero," I said.

"Like you," she said.

"About that," I said, looking away. "There's something I need to confess."

"That duffel wasn't for Kaye, was it?" she asked.

"No, it wasn't," I said. "I owe you an apology."

"You almost pulled a runaway bride," she said. "I don't think I'm the one you should be apologizing to."

I groaned. I'd need talk to Ceff. I wasn't looking forward to that conversation. But if he too had guessed that I'd decided to run, then I owed him an explanation.

"Not for running," I said. "I promised no more secrets. At least, when I'm not cursed or under a geas or legally bound not to tell a human vassal."

"How weird is it that you said all of that with a totally straight face?" she asked.

"On a scale of one to ten?" I said. "It doesn't even rate."

"Thank you," she said. "For telling me. For coming back. For no more secrets."

"No more secrets," I said with a nod. "Now where is my favorite little night-mare?"

Jinx shook a toy moon that had a star-shaped bell dangling from it and Fernvolg came trotting out from behind my desk.

"Hi, Fernie," I said, voice gentle. "You hungry?"

The night-mare bounded toward me and I backed up, holding my hands in the air.

"I think she likes you," Jinx said.

"Or she's hungry," I said. "Although she looks much healthier than she did when we found her."

Fernvolg's fur was shiny and lustrous and her galaxy-filled eyes glowed with starlight.

"I doubt she's hungry," Jinx said. "I haven't had a scary dream since she arrived, neither has Forneus. Not sure why that makes him nervous, but I for one am enjoying the lack of nightmares."

I grabbed a leash from the hook beside the door. It was a dog's leash, probably meant for a mastiff or a chubby boxer, not a horse's bridle. But Ceff had flinched at anything resembling a bridle at the pet store and I wasn't keen with putting a bit inside a night-mare's mouth. This would have to do.

"Think that'll hold her?" Jinx asked.

"Doubtful," I said. "But it'll help with the illusion that I'm out with my dog and keep people from interfering."

Of course, Fernie might end up ripping off my arm or dragging me along behind her like a kite. I had no idea if the night-mare would tolerate being on a leash, even if it was just for keeping up appearances, but I was about to find out.

"Fernie, want to go for walkies?" I asked, shaking the leash.

She nudged me with her nose and nearly knocked me on my butt, pawing at the end of the leash.

"I think that's a yes," Jinx said, laughing.

"Who's a good girl?" I cooed to Fernie, ignoring Jinx. I clipped the leash to her collar, which was covered in silver stars, and gave a tentative step toward the door. So far, so good. "Who's the bestest girl?"

"Ivy?" Jinx asked.

I turned and shot her a questioning glance, hand on the door.

"No matter what I happens, I need you to remember something," she said.

"What's that?" I asked.

"We're stronger together."

CHAPTER 42

Jinx's words rang in my ears as I walked Fernie up the cobblestone street. We had a long walk ahead of us, plenty of time to mull over what was quickly becoming my best friend's new mantra.

We're stronger together.

I had to believe that, especially now. Frost-rimed windows and the rainbow shimmer on patches of sidewalk hastened my step, my heart beating faster. I fought the urge to run, to try to save my friends by fleeing the city and everything I've built here. But Jinx was right.

We're stronger together.

Even before Gaius had strode into Private Eye with his demands and dusty temper tantrum, I'd been feeling off-balance. That was due in large part to the ghosts in the room, the loved ones we now missed. My father had left to protect us from the curse he carried, but he wasn't the only person whose absence was like a hole in my gut.

As a young woman, I'd had only two people I trusted with my secret. Jinx had been the first and she'd grown to become like a sister to me. The other was Kaye O'Shay, a powerful witch and a hero of Harborsmouth.

I'd come to rely on Kaye for wisdom and guidance. Though she'd been prickly, made a bundle selling me protection charms, and was an insatiable prankster, Kaye had become a part of my new family. Her loss was a deep wound that I hoped to heal, for me and for everyone who had grown to love her.

Sometimes, it surprised me how much Kaye's apprentice missed her. The old witch had been a harsh teacher and an incorrigible trickster, but Arachne loved her. And, like me, the kid felt somewhat responsible for Kaye's current predicament.

After the battle in Kaye's spell kitchen, Arachne had called the one group of people able to subdue and contain a powerful witch. The teen had stepped up and reached out to The Circle, a witch coven led by her mother, that operated a facility outside of town that was part hospital and part prison.

If anyone could sneak Fernie inside the asylum and help us break Kaye out of there, it was Arachne.

I pulled out my phone and gave her a call.

"Hey, Ivy," Arachne said, turning down the music that nearly blasted out my eardrums and made Fernie look at me like I was nuts. "What's up? If you need protection charms, you'll have to wait until the weekend. All I've got is some sage."

"That's okay, that's not why I called," I said.

"Pizza party?" she asked, with a hopeful lilt.

"Maybe later," I said. "You busy right now?"

"Not really," she said. "What's up?"

"Think you can meet me at the asylum?" I asked.

"Sure, but why now?" she asked. She paused, probably checking the time. "It's too early for visiting hours."

"Because," I said. "We're going to break Kaye out of there."

"Be there in ten," she said.

Arachne ended the call. I looked down at Fernie, waddling along at my side.

"We better hurry, sweetie," I said in a sing-song voice. "We don't want to keep auntie Arachne waiting."

CHAPTER 43

"**Y**ou need me to sneak you in, to a heavily guarded asylum, with a farting unicorn?" Arachne asked.

Fernie harrumphed and snorted in the young witch's direction, unimpressed.

"Yep," I said. "And, for the record, Fernie here is a night-mare, not a unicorn. The bestest little night-mare, right, Fernie?"

Arachne glanced wide-eyed at Fernie then back at me, folding her arms across her chest. She was wearing her signature purple and black, from the dyed streak in her otherwise blond hair to her ringer t-shirt and Chuck Taylor's.

"Okay, fine," she said. "But you owe me, like, a lot of pizza."

"Done," I said, nodding.

Arachne sighed and turned to look up at the stone and brick asylum that rose from the manicured lawn at our feet.

"Any ideas how to get us inside?" I asked.

"You could pretend to be sick, but..." she said.

"But?" I asked.

"But your aura is, like, glowing," she said, waving a hand. "You're bursting with power, which I want to hear about later by the way. Problem is, the nurses and orderlies will never believe you're sick or injured with that aura."

Well, crap. I didn't think I'd see the day when I was too healthy for a mission. I frowned, searching the building for another way inside.

Fernie belched and farted, and Arachne groaned.

"Ew, gross," she said, nose wrinkling. "What have you been feeding her?"

"Necromancer dreams," I said. Arachne narrowed her eyes and I held up gloved hands. "Hey, not my fault. It wasn't my doing. That's just how we found her. The only thing alive enough to dream in that place was a lich king."

It said something for Arachne's upbringing and her recent employment at The Emporium that all she did was shrug at the mention of a lich king.

"I suppose that makes sense, because she smells like death," she said, waving a hand in front of her face. "Maybe they make Pepto for night-mares?"

That gave me an idea.

"Wait," I said, smiling. "Do they treat magic animals here?"

"Like, familiars and stuff?" she asked. "Yes, sometimes."

"Good," I said. "I have an idea."

CHAPTER 44

Antiseptic and medicinal scents mixed with the smoky smell of burning sage, tickling my nose. That is until Fernie let out another putrid fart.

"Good girl," I said.

The night-mare tossed her head, looking proud of herself.

"She doesn't need to act sick anymore," Arachne said, chewing on a purple strand of hair.

Our ruse had worked, and it was all thanks to Fernie and her flatulent tummy issues. But pretending to be here for an emergency witchy veterinary exam could only get us so far. Now we needed stealth and cunning and a whopping dose of luck.

"Shhh!" I whispered, holding a gloved finger to my lips.

We crouched in a stairwell, waiting for the echo of shoes on linoleum to fade away. I inched forward, straining to listen for sounds, but all I heard was the distant beep of medical machinery and Fernie's stomach rumbling.

I held my breath and inched to the corner. I risked a peek, relieved to see the hallway was empty.

"Okay, clear," I said.

Arachne nodded, and we crab-walked our way to Kaye's hospital room, careful to keep below the small windows set into the top half of the doors we passed. My skin tingled and I tried to ignore the grids of silver and iron mesh set into the glass, but it was a relief when we reached Kaye's room.

We slid inside, me in the lead and Fernie between us, and I let out the air I'd been holding. The room held a bed and a chair. Kaye was sleeping on the bed with a gorgeous black cat curled up on her stomach, guarding my friend, protecting her from harm.

"Hey, Midnight," I said.

My heart swelled. I'd visited as often as I could, but I hadn't realized until now just how much I'd missed Kaye and her feline familiar. I moved to the bed and stroked Midnight behind the ears while the cat eyed Fernie.

The night-mare bowed prettily, farted, and snickered. Midnight gave Fernie a regal glance and started to purr.

"Huh, I guess they're going to be friends," Arachne said, chewing on her hair. "What now?"

Arachne was nervous. She wasn't the only one. There was so much riding on this. What if we couldn't cure Kaye?

On the way here, planning our way inside, I'd started to let myself hope that this would work. Staging a rescue sounded great in theory, but it didn't do any good if we couldn't help Kaye break through her trauma and wake up. Hope and fear sucked the air from the room, making me dizzy. I was setting myself up for disappointment on an epic scale.

"Think she'll be, you know, scary Kaye when she wakes up?" Arachne asked, flicking a furtive glance at our sleeping friend.

"Oberon's eyes, I hope not," I said, a prickle of unease skittering across my scalp.

Kaye and I hadn't left things on the best of terms. Before she was brought to the asylum, she'd tried to kill me.

"Maybe, you should wait in the hall," I said. "Keep an eye out for orderlies."

Arachne nodded, her relief evident as she hurried toward the door. She muttered a prayer, something to the Goddess, and ducked into the hall. I turned back to join the adorable night-mare at my side.

"Okay, Fernie," I said. "This is Kaye. She's my friend, and she needs our help. You hungry, pretty girl?"

Midnight watched us, tail flicking, and I held my breath.

Fernie waddled closer and touched her silver and black horn to Kaye's ashen hand. The tattoos that traced my friend's fingers pulsated, reacting to the night-mare's magic. Fernie's eyes swirled, constellations spinning mesmerizingly, and I had to take a step back away from the bed and shake my head to clear away the fog of sleep.

Whatever the night-mare was doing, it definitely had a field of influence. Even Midnight, perched on Kaye's slowly rising and falling stomach, yawned, showing off sharp, tiny teeth. Where Midnight was a sleek and beautiful predator,

Fernie was an elegant devourer of dreams. For the hundredth time today, I hoped that was a good thing.

Kaye's eyelids fluttered and her body shuddered convulsively. Fingers crossed that was a good sign. To keep from panicking, I turned to the night-mare and tried to give her some encouragement.

"Who's a good girl?" I asked, cooing at her.

Fernie's tummy growled followed by a noisy fart. That's my girl.

"You're such a stinky, pinky, wittle precious, aren't you, sweetie?" I asked.

Fernie lifted her star-filled eyes to me and whinnied.

"I do hope you aren't speaking to me, dear," Kaye said.

I stood speechless. Thankfully, Arache must have been watching through the window in the room's door.

"Kaye!" she squealed, rushing into the room.

"What are you girls doing?" Kaye asked.

"Rescuing you," Arachne said.

"We're breaking you out of here," I said, nodding my agreement.

"Ah, well, good," Kaye said. She squinted at me, gazing an inch or two off my shoulder, then looking down at Fernie. "You've been busy, I see."

I shoved my hands into my pockets.

"Fought some zombies, killed a lich king, stole his night-mare," I said, looking away. "The usual."

"While I would greatly like to hear about your adventures, I do think I would like to go home," she said.

"Funny you should say that," Arachne said, wheeling over a wheelchair.

Midnight leapt down onto the chair's seat, inspected it, and turned to nod his approval. I guess this mode of escape passed the cat's inspection. Good thing, since Kaye had been bedbound for weeks and we needed to hurry the heck out of here.

When Kaye had been admitted to the asylum, she'd been in the thrall of powerful magic. But the woman in the bed before me was my old friend, not an enemy. I'd bet my life on it.

If we got caught by The Circle's operatives, it just might come to that.

CHAPTER 45

Sneaking out of the asylum took steady nerves and more than one magic spell. Good thing we had two witches with us. It also helped that Arachne had spent plenty of time here at her mother's side, making her intimately familiar with The Circle's security protocols. That inside knowledge gave us the edge we needed to escape, or so we hoped.

"Look, we're nearly home safe, but we still need to get past those guards," I said. "Any ideas?"

We'd had to leave the wheelchair on the second-floor landing, opting for slower movement rather than face the nursing station head-on. But that meant trying to tiptoe down a stairwell with a frightened teenager, a frail woman, a cat, and a farting night-mare.

"We need a distraction," Arachne said. "A big one."

"Fireball?" I asked.

I could cast a fireball. But that left us with the problem of managing enough of a fire for a distraction, but not so big as to cause damage or casualties. I'd need to tap into a ley line for that level of power and control, something that might tip off the asylum's witch security.

"Too risky," she said.

"What about a monster, dear?" Kaye asked, stroking her cat.

I swear she was enjoying this.

"You can't summon here," Arachne said, scowling. "The entire place is warded against calling monsters."

"Leave that to me, my dear," Kaye said. "And to Midnight."

She set the black cat down on the linoleum-tiled floor.

"Glamour?" I asked.

I suppose the old with could probably cast a glamour on the cat, making it look terrifying long enough to distract the guards and let us escape. Maybe.

"Better that you not know the specifics," Kaye said with a wink.

Oh, yeah. She was definitely enjoying this. But maybe Kaye was right. Plausible deniability and all that.

"Um, okay," Arachne said. "Wait for my signal."

Arachne strode out toward the front doors, leaving me to gape at her. The kid was brave, I'd give her that.

"Stay with me," I said, glancing down at Fernie.

The night-mare whinnied and nodded her head. Kaye dropped Midnight to the ground and I held my breath. Arachne spoke with the guards at the door, acting for all the world like a bored teenaged.

Her minor distraction gave the cat an opportunity to slip across the gap and behind the reception desk.

"What now?" I asked, keeping my voice low.

"We wait," Kaye said.

A dark shape, Midnight I presumed, crept out from the other side of the reception desk, slid across the far side of the lobby, and disappeared into the lobby level ward. I wondered idly how long we'd have to wait for Kaye's spell.

We didn't have to wait long.

Screams erupted from the opposite wing of the hospital, drawing the door guards into the ward and the chaos beyond. Whatever Kaye had used for a glamour on Midnight, it had to be terrifying. Too bad I wouldn't have a chance to find out.

Arachne waved us forward, and we ran across the lobby. Luck was for once with us. We crept out the front doors and ran down the path that led to the front gates. Screams continued behind us, and I bit my lip.

Would Midnight be okay?

I needn't have worried. As we ran down the path, green lawn blurring in my peripheral vision, we were joined by a ball of black fur. Midnight had made it out safely.

In fact, so had we.

I turned to Arachne when we finally hurried through the gates and down a side alley, out of sight of the asylum's grounds.

"Thank you," I said, dragging air into oxygen-deprived lungs. "We couldn't have done this without you."

"Just, like, don't think this is over," she said, eyes darting furtively over her shoulder. "My mother doesn't give up that easily. Neither does The Circle."

Eventually, we'd have to face The Circle, and Arachne's mother's wrath, but by then, I hoped that Kaye would be healthy and stable enough to prove that she was no longer a threat to herself or others. Until then, she wanted to go home.

I could understand that desire. Sadly, Kaye's physical home, The Emporium, was mostly rubble and ash. Arachne chewed on a purple lock of hair and eyed Kaye warily. Neither of us knew how much Kaye remembered from our battle, nor how much she might have heard of our conversations while she slept.

Now that we were away from the asylum and drawing closer to the street in the Old Port Quarter where Kaye had lived for over a century, I was trying to broach the subject. But we'd waited too long to fill Kaye in on the details. Neither of us had expected the older woman, who'd spent recent weeks in a hospital bed, to start running. We hurried to catch up, Fernie at my heels. Even the night-mare tried to hurry. But we were too late.

CHAPTER 46

Kaye flung herself around the stone and brick corner and gasped, a tattooed hand flying up to cover her mouth. She hugged Midnight close to her chest with her other hand, as if sheltering the cat from the cold, hard truth.

"What have I done?" Kaye muttered. "How could I...?"

Kaye blanched, shame and sorrow dancing across her face.

"This is my fault," I said, shaking my head.

"But I..." she said.

"No," I said. "This is on me. And I have a plan to rebuild The Emporium. I've got this."

"Dear Goddess, what about Marvin, and Hob?" she asked, voice quivering. "Are they hurt?"

"They're fine," Arachne said, staring down at her purple shoes. "Ivy found them a place to stay. Just like she'll help you."

The kid had more faith in me than I did, but I swore not to let her, or Kaye, down again.

"I have something to show you," I said.

"I don't know how much more of this I can take right now," Kaye said, sagging.

She looked exhausted. Midnight licked her hand, trying to comfort her.

"Don't worry," I said. "It's something good. Think you can walk a little further?"

Kaye took a deep breath, holding Midnight close. She seemed to draw strength from the black cat. Maybe, she did. I didn't really know the inner workings of the relationship between a witch and her familiar. If nothing else, Midnight's affection appeared to give her comfort.

"Yes," she whispered.

Arachne gave her teacher an encouraging smile, and we continued walking along the sidewalk, Fernie trotting along happily on her leash. Midnight snuck an occasional glance at the night-mare, and I had the nagging suspicion that those two might really become friends. Maybe, when the repair work on The Emporium was done, Fernie might find a home there.

I'm not sure if Hob would return or continue to live in Eden Park. I wasn't even sure if he'd welcome the witch back into his heart. But we were about to find out.

"What is this place?" Kaye asked, blinking at the gardens that had sprung up from the Wild Hunt's fallen. "Or rather, what happened here? This was an industrial park."

We stood on the sidewalk just outside Eden Park. This would be a strange homecoming for Kaye, but I could ease her discomfort with the knowledge that something good had come from our city's recent battles.

"Arachne, think you can talk to the pooka guards about letting us through?" I asked. "I'd like a minute with Kaye."

"Sure," she said, raising an eyebrow.

"If they give you any trouble, ask for Marvin," I said. "Or holler for me. But try not to tell Marvin why we're here. I'd like it to be a surprise."

"Okay," she said.

Arachne nodded and marched over to Violet and Amber. The pookas were still guarding the entrance, or having a dance party. With those two, it was hard to tell.

Midnight eyed the pookas, tail twitching.

"No eating the faeries," I said.

The cat hissed at me and went back to licking Kaye's hand.

"Why are there so many fae here?" Kaye asked. "Not that I should be surprised. They are drawn to you."

"To me?" I squeaked. "Nah, I just have a thing for strays. Nobody should be without a home. Or friends."

"I suppose I am one of your strays now, dear," Kaye said. "How the wands have turned."

I shifted my weight and rubbed the back of my neck.

"Um, we'll find a place for you stay," I said. "And I'll rebuild The Emporium. Until then, I do hope you'll let us help. We can figure this out, together."

Kaye nodded, kissing Midnight and making the cat purr.

"Do not worry about me, dear," she said. "I have a place I can lay my head while we rebuild. Yes, we. I'm not such an old fool as to think I can do this on my own. Not anymore."

"Thank you," I said, letting out a relieved breath.

"For what, dear?" she asked.

"For trusting me," I said. "For letting me help."

"Don't thank me yet," she said, a sly twinkle in her eye. "You don't know what I'm about to ask of you."

My shoulders slid back, and I lifted my chin, ready for whatever Kaye might throw at me.

"I owe you," I said. "And you're my friend. What do you need?"

"A temporary home for Midnight," she said.

"Is that all?" I asked, grinning. "Of course. Absolutely. Midnight can stay with me. The loft is super crowded, and I'm not sure how a cat might feel about a curious demon toddler, but Fernie is bunking in our office, and they seem to get along."

It would mean another trip to the pet store. Maybe, we'd get Midnight and Fernie matching beds. That would be adorable.

"He is a cat, but more than a cat," she said, staring down into Midnight's eyes.

Because he was a witch's familiar? I was curious, but Arachne was waving for us to join her.

"Um, okay," I said. "So, anything special I should know about?"

"I am sure Midnight will behave himself," Kaye said. "Won't you, dear?"

I could have sworn the cat winked at me, a smug grin on its lips. Great. That was just great.

"Why am not convinced?" I muttered.

"Just don't do anything foolish, my dear," Kaye said.

"Like?" I asked.

"Like invite over any of your pooka friends," she said.

"Oh, sure," I said, watching as Midnight ran a pink tongue over tiny, sharp teeth. Why did I feel like I'd invited a furry vampire into my home? "That would probably be bad."

"And don't leave shiny things lying around the place," she said. "Not unless you wish for Midnight to keep them safe for you."

Oh, joy. The cat sounded like Hob. I'd have to cat-proof our office before letting Midnight have free reign. I suppose if anything sparkly went missing, I'd know where to look.

"Okay," I said. "Good to know."

I tried to think of anything specific we might need to know. Like allergies, or dietary requirements. It's not like I could feed a cat pizza. What do cats eat? Fish? Steak?

"Does he eat meat?" I asked.

"Oh, yes," she said, a grin tugging at her lips.

"Cool," I said, a chill skittering up my spine.

Kaye sure could be spooky sometimes.

"And this place?" she asked, deftly changing the subject. "These gardens that Arachne is so eager for us to enter, how did a park come to be here?"

"It sprang from the Wild Hunt's fallen," I said, glad for the change of subject. "This is where we held our last stand."

"So much blood," Kaye whispered. "So many lives sacrificed."

"That's why it's important to preserve this place," I said, heart swelling. I would not let those we lost to have died in vain. "To protect it. These gardens are a sanctuary for the more peaceful fae. For the marginalized and the displaced. What better way to honor the memories of those who gave their lives to protect this city?"

"What better way, indeed," she said. "You've done well here."

"Well, it's not really like I can take the credit," I said, rubbing the back of my neck. "We have the Wild Hunt to thank for the gardens, not me. I just had some ideas of what they could be used for. That's all."

"No, that's not true," she said. "You are the true reason these gardens sprouted."

"I don't follow," I said, frowning.

"You've been tugging at the ley lines from the moment your faerie powers awakened," Kaye said.

I wanted to deny it, but she had a point.

"I guess," I said, chewing the inside of my cheek. "A few times. When the situation was extreme enough, I've tapped into their power. I try not to make a habit of it. Ley lines give me a killer headache and make my teeth feel like they're going to fall out."

"But you have made a habit of it, dear," she said. "And you will continue to reach for the ley lines, no matter how dire the circumstance. You, Ivy, are a natural conduit."

Arachne tried to get our attention, but I focused on Kaye. She was rarely this loquacious, and I needed answers.

"But a conduit to what?" I asked. "To power? To magic?"

"To Faerie," she said.

"What does that mean?" I asked. "Being a conduit to Faerie?"

"It means, dear," she said. "That you are the one person able to renew the bonds between the human world and Faerie."

That didn't sound terrifying or anything.

"And if I don't want to?" I asked.

"You've already begun," she said, nodding toward Arachne and strolling across the street.

"Awesome," I said.

"It's not all bad," she said. "There will be change, of course, as Faerie's magic returns to this world, but you aren't just altering magic. You are bringing our two realms closer together."

"Like a human-faerie ambassador?" I asked.

"You are already that, my dear," she said.

"So, when you say that I'm bringing the two realms closer together, you mean that literally?" I asked, lifting my hands wide and sliding them closer together to demonstrate my meaning.

"Yes," she said. "You are, for want of a better term, changing and shifting the fabric of the universe."

"Damn," I muttered. "I really am tugging on the threads between our worlds."

"For good or ill, yes," she said.

It was a lot to take in. My mind raced with the possibilities, most of them bad. But if I brought our worlds together, hopefully without cataclysmically colliding, then I might be able to reopen the doors to Faerie.

That could have horrific consequences, but there was one positive that I could immediately think of. Torn and the others would be able to honor their dead with a proper burial. No more burying cat sidhe in our pet cemeteries. It was a silver lining to hold on to.

CHAPTER 47

Prison breaks, or in this case an asylum break, aren't easy. If anyone tries to say otherwise, they probably have a bridge to sell you. But curing Kaye, seeing her free, and reuniting our weird little family helped ease the turmoil roiling inside me since my trip to the Necropolis.

I should be exhausted. Instead, I was more energized than I'd been in weeks.

It helped that Hob and Marvin had welcomed Kaye back with open arms. Sure, Hob had acted grouchy at first, but it was all a ruse. It wasn't long before he lost his frown and was dancing a merry jig. Even the gnomes and pookas joined in, swarming around Kaye in a riot of excited squeals and peals of laughter.

Their laughter was contagious. Even Delilah was giggling as Violet and Amber treated her bosom like a bouncy castle, a trick that held Torn's rapt attention. I'd been reluctant to invite the succubus to join us, but, so far, she hadn't sucked anyone's life force.

We were safe, for now.

Marvin had set aside his club and discarded his armor, looking once more like a happy, awkward teenager as he danced with Arachne. I was saddened that they ever had to grow up, but for today at least, they could shed that weight and enjoy Kaye's homecoming.

Seeing all my friends together in one place warmed my heart. It also helped me make a decision.

Since Faerie's painful forced attempt at my transformation in the Necropolis, and Kaye's terrifying words about my effect on our worlds and the ley lines, I'd started mulling over possibilities and the reality of our current situation.

We faced constant challenges and frequent horrors. If Mab continued her efforts to throw her twisted pets at me, it was only going to get worse.

I'd decided to stay, to remain here in Harborsmouth with the people I loved. Seeing them all around me, happy and whole, helped me make another difficult choice.

I had sworn to protect this city and its innocent human and faerie inhabitants. I'd promised to do whatever it took to keep my friends and family safe. If there was anything I could do to ensure their safety, I would do it. No matter how large the personal sacrifice.

My heart swelled. I turned to Jinx and smiled.

"This calls for a celebration," I said.

"Wait, you're the one who wants a party?" Jinx asked. "Who are you and what did you do with my best friend?"

"Hey, I didn't agree to a bacchanal, just a simple gathering of friends," I said, holding up gloved hands, palm out.

"No take backs?" she asked.

"Nope," I said. "But it needs to be tonight."

So many of my loved ones were already here enjoying themselves. Who knew when that might happen again? You never know when disaster is going to strike.

We'd have a party, and I could share my decision with them all.

"Can we have cake?" she asked.

"There should definitely be cake," I said.

"Dancing?" she asked.

I looked around us. Half of my friends were dancing already. If we gave them sugar, I'm pretty sure there'd be no stopping them.

"Sure," I said with a shrug. "Why not?"

"You should go to weird zombie pocket dimensions more often," she said, getting out her phone and sending a flurry of text messages.

I shook my head and left Jinx to party planning. I had preparations of my own.

CHAPTER 48

"A toast," I said, raising a glass of mead. "To friends."

The fermented honey drink was popular with every faerie present. Considering we were throwing a party in Eden Park, a magic garden filled with pookas, we'd probably go through barrels of the stuff. It would be worth the cost.

"To coming home," Ceff said.

"To family," I said.

Everyone was here. Even the faces of those who couldn't be present in body, like my father Skyping in on Torn's phone and Skillywidden reflected in the surface of the small pond where I stood. Each of their faces mirrored the love I'd come to feel for my chosen family. I would die for every one of them. But, for the first time in ages, I didn't think I had to.

Jinx was right. We were stronger together. No matter what Faerie's claim on me meant for the future and no matter what monsters Mab threw at us, we would prevail. We had to.

I was done losing the people that I loved.

"You okay, lass?" Hob asked.

"I know what I need to do," I said.

In the end, it was all about choice. Everything important was about choice. I'd chosen my family. Jinx and I chose to be sisters and so we were. Ceff and I chose to love and trust each other and now we were betrothed. Sparky and I chose our bond, for me to be his safe place, and now he was my son. Even becoming a hero had been due to a series of choices.

"Ivy?" Marvin asked, shuffling large feet.

"It's okay, dear," Kaye said. "This is her destiny."

Icy tendrils of magic slithered across the small pond. Frost rimed the water's surface, but concentric circles rippled at its center, pulsing to the beat of my heart.

"Am I hallucinating?" Jinx asked. "Please tell me I'm hallucinating."

"She made a Choice," Forneus said, coming to stand at Jinx's side.

"What?" Jinx asked, sounding horrified and clutching Sparky to her chest.

"My heart and the heart of Faerie are one," I said. "I'm pretty sure they always were. I just didn't realize it until now."

"That's because you had to choose it, princess," Torn said.

"The lass be more than a princess now," Hob said, voice barely a whisper.

A crown broke the surface of the icy pond, held aloft by the hand of a creature so beautiful it hurt to look directly at her. I'd never seen a high elf. If the lore was correct, the elvish nobility had left Faerie and the human realm long ago. But the thing I remember being told about elves was that they were an extension of the land, manifestations in the form of Faerie. It was probably a good thing that they were gone. If elves really did look anything like Faerie, we'd spend our days enthralled by them, because Faerie was too gorgeous for words.

Instead, I focused on the object in her hands. I hadn't seen it from this vantage point before. I'd felt the burning of the ice and the piercing of its thorns, but I hadn't seen the elegant weave of icy vines and frozen roses. It was beautiful and deadly as befit a queen of Faerie.

"Is this what you really want?" Ceff asked.

"Yes," I said, a tear running down my cheek. It wasn't like before, back in the Necropolis. This wasn't a prison sentence being meted out by an outside force. I wasn't frozen in place and my tears were lukewarm rather than razor-sharp chips of ice. The choice was mine to make. "I choose this."

Ceff nodded and took a step back to stand at my shoulder. His message was clear. He would not stop me, in this or in any of my decisions. My choices would always be my own.

"You can do this," he said. "I believe in you."

For the first time in a long time, I believed in me too.

IVY GRANGER WORLD

Don't miss these great books set in the world of Ivy Granger.

Ivy Ganger, Psychic Detective Series

Frostbite: Short Story

Ivy Granger can see the monsters walking the streets of Harborsmouth.
Vampires, faeries, demons? No problem. Too bad Ivy Granger's new client needs help with deadly ghosts.

Shadow Sight

Welcome to Harborsmouth, where monsters walk the streets unseen by humans...except those with second sight, like Ivy Granger.

Blood and Mistletoe: An Ivy Granger Novella

Holidays are worse than a full moon for making people crazy. In Harborsmouth, where many of the residents are undead vampires or monstrous fae, the combination may prove deadly.

Ghost Light

Holidays are worse than a full moon for making people crazy. In Harborsmouth, where many of the residents are undead vampires or monstrous fae, the combination may prove deadly.

Club Nexus: An Ivy Granger Novella

A demon, an Unseelie faerie, and a vampire walk into a bar...

Burning Bright

Burning down the house...

Devil in the Details: Short Story

Sparky, the adorable lop-eared demon, gets into trouble in this Ivy Granger short story originally published in The Final Summons anthology.

Birthright

Being a faerie princess isn't all it's cracked up to be...

Hound's Bite

Ivy Granger thought she left the worst of Mab's creations behind when she escaped Faerie. She thought wrong.

Thrill on Joysen Hill: Short Story

Few places are as rife with opportunity or as fraught with danger as Harborsmouth's notorious Joysen Hill, but when Torn gets stuck babysitting, he can only think of one place in Harborsmouth interesting enough to take a demon toddler, a teenage bridge troll, and a grouchy hearth brownie.

Blood Rite

Ivy Granger psychic detective takes on a simple grave robbing case, but in Harborsmouth nothing is ever simple when dealing with the dead.

Tales from Harborsmouth

A collection of Ivy Granger short stories and novellas. Demons, faeries, vampires, and wererats—anything is possible in Harborsmouth.

Hunters' Guild Series

Hunting in Bruges

The only thing worse than being a Hunter in the fae-ridden city of Harborsmouth, is hunting vampires in Bruges.

Whitechapel Paranormal Society Series

Craven Street

Much maligned by their male counterparts within the S.P.R.B., the women of the Whitechapel Paranormal Society are on their own to face a sinister dark mastermind as dismembered bodies are set across London's East End like figures on a game board. Can they predict the killer's next move—a bloody, ritualistic murder that might tip the scales and give demons dominion over all of London—before he strikes again?

Ebooks, Trade Paperbacks, Audiobooks

Ivy Granger Psychic Detective books are available in ebook, trade paperback, and audio. Look for the Whispersync for Voice symbol for special Audible and Kindle discounts.
Visit EJStevensAuthor.com , Ivy Granger.com, and WhitechapelParanormal.com to listen to free audiobook samples, interviews with the narrators, and more.

Get Lost in Translations

Ivy Granger books are available worldwide in multiple languages.
Visit EJStevensAuthor.com to learn more and get lost in translations.

Freebies

Visit the Freebies Page at EJStevensAuthor.com for free audiobook samples, Ivy Granger ringtones, wallpapers, and more!
Want a free book and access to ARCs, exclusive news, and giveaways?
Sign up for E.J.'s newsletter.

COMING SOON TO THE WORLD OF IVY GRANGER

Ivy Granger, Psychic Detective

Watertight

When Torn is accused of murdering a local mermaid, Ivy Granger is plunged into the deep end of water fae politics.

Dressed in White

Something old, something new, something borrowed, and something blue...

Whitechapel Paranormal Society

Eeper Weeper

The tedium and terrors of Josephine "Jo" Hadley's existence within the stone walls of London's Bethnal Asylum are interrupted by a strange visitor, Cora Drummond. Will Jo Hadley's unusual talent for inciting prophetic nursery rhymes prove useful to the crown?

One for Sorrow

Demons and necromancers went into hiding within the labyrinthine warrens of Whitechapel, but after three years of secretly feasting on the souls of London's East End they are back stronger than ever before. Will the Whitechapel Paranormal Society rise up from the ashes of the S.P.R.B., or will all of London become the Devil's playground?

ABOUT THE AUTHOR

E.J. Stevens is the bestselling, award-winning author of the
IVY GRANGER, PSYCHIC DETECTIVE urban fantasy series,
the SPIRIT GUIDE young adult series, the HUNTERS' GUILD
urban fantasy series, and the WHITECHAPEL
PARANORMAL SOCIETY Victorian Gothic horror series. She
is known for filling pages with quirky characters, bloodsucking
vampires, psychotic faeries, and snarky, kick-butt heroines.
Her novels are available worldwide in multiple languages.

BTS Red Carpet Award winner for Best Novel, Raven Award
winner for Best Urban Fantasy, Imadjinn Award winner for
Best Short Story, Independent Audiobook Award winner for
Best Short Story, SYAE finalist for Best Paranormal Series,
Best Novella, and Best Horror, winner of the PRG Reviewer's
Choice Award for Best Paranormal Fantasy Novel, Best Young
Adult Paranormal Series, Best Urban Fantasy Novel, and
finalist for Best Young Adult Paranormal Novel and Best
Urban Fantasy Series.

When E.J. isn't at her writing desk, she enjoys dancing along
seaside cliffs, singing in graveyards, and sleeping in faerie
circles. E.J. currently resides in a magical forest on the coast of
Maine where she finds daily inspiration for her writing.

CONNECT WITH E.J. STEVENS

Twitter: @EJStevensAuthor
Website: www.EJStevensAuthor.com
Blog: www.FromtheShadows.info